beneath pale water

beneath pale water

Thalia Henry

CLOUD
INK

First published in 2017
Published by Cloud Ink Press Ltd, Auckland
P.O. Box 8988, Symonds Street, Auckland, 1150
www.cloudink.co.nz

ISBN 978-0-473-40726-1

Cover artwork: Rosa-May Rutherford

Cover design, book design and typesetting: Craig Violich (cvdgraphics.nz)
Printed by IngramSpark

Published with the support of Creative New Zealand

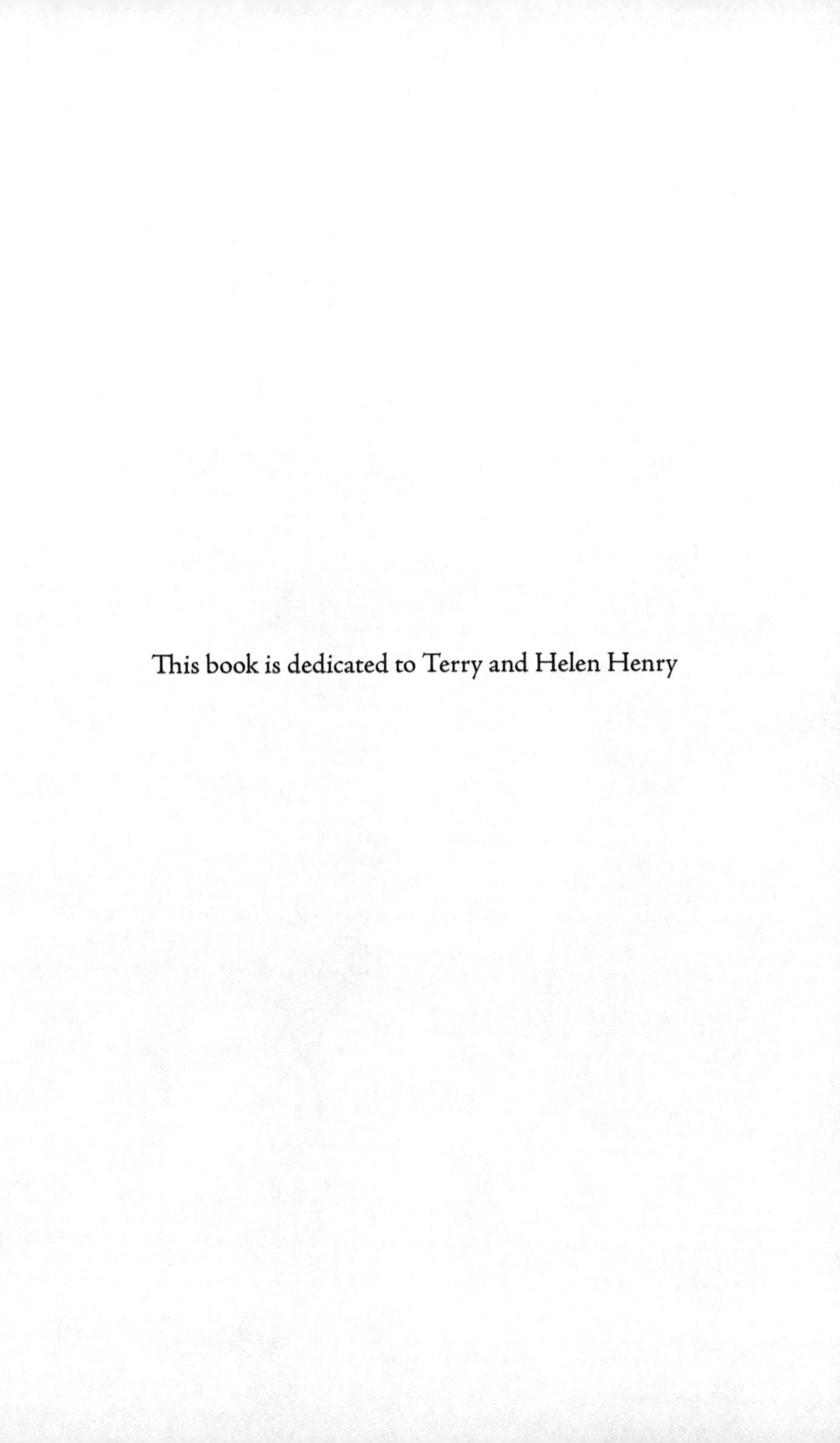

This book is dedicated to Terry and Helen Henry

SUMMER

When I die, I'll be a bird. I'll fly over lakes and mountains. Another bird will fly beside me. Sometimes we'll wheel in circles just to get a closer look at the grassy hillocks and cadences of the water. Everyday we'll see the curve of the earth; green, blue, opalescent skies. All of this will be in silence. Sweet silence. It won't matter if we're lost. Why? You wonder . . . because the whole world will be our home, with Otago at the centre. With my wing tip I'll be able to touch something precious, and pure and true. A bird's life may be fragile but I can imagine no other life so perfect.

Freedom. Freedom is the air beneath our wings raising our silhouettes by delicate wisps of lift that take heat from the winding roads. Freedom is the crisp texture of unpolluted surroundings. Freedom is circling amongst these invisible columns and currents along ridges of mountains and beyond to empty spaces never before occupied and untainted by prying eyes.

1

A hawk was circling, majestic, powerful and free. Delia's feet dangled idly in the chill of Lake Aviemore, her eyes looking up at the sky where the hawk cast a shadow against the hills. She traced its outline, her hand quivering, then pulled her feet out of the water and hugged her knees. In the sun, her skin warmed, and she left the lake to fly with the hawk. She followed the jagged line of the hills, swinging in a tandem dance. As she rose upwards her sight cleared. She swept above grassy hillocks and cadences of water, the curve of the earth, green, blue, opalescent skies. All in silence she flew. Sweet silence.

The sound of an object piercing the water disturbed her reverie. She turned her head and recognised a young man standing further along the shore, skipping stones into the lake. He hadn't been around for a while and he looked different. She knew he'd grown up on an orchard not so far from here. For a moment he reminded her of Ben and her breath caught in her throat. But Ben was gone, she told herself. Ben was gone. Her cheeks were damp and her eyes watery; she wiped them clear hoping that from where he stood he wouldn't have noticed.

Neither of them talked at first and the silence between them became accepted. The man faced the sunset and the lake. He continued to skip stones. She watched him for a time. His stance and his stare were focused, concentrated on his task as if aiming for a specific target that she couldn't see. She squinted against the glare.

'I came here to get away,' she said.

He turned towards her. 'From what?'

'People.'

'So did I.' He grinned and held out a dusty hand.

'Luke,' he said.

She took his hand, studying him. 'I know who you are.'

He wore a loose cotton shirt and rolled up jeans above olive skinned feet stained with dirt. His straggly hair was lightened by the sun and the tan of his skin contrasted with green eyes. The outline of his chin was shadowed with a light beard, one he hadn't had before.

He smiled, released her hand and sat down beside her.

'You ran away, right?' she said. 'That's what everyone's been saying.'

He seemed not to hear the comment, picked up a stone and placed it in his palm, then added a second and a third. The stones were smooth and flat and he piled them into a pyramid. He was so absorbed in the task that he remained quiet for a time. His wrists were wrapped with a few cotton bracelets that had lost their colour; his clothes were faded, earth-toned, dust was ingrained in the pores of his skin.

The cairn became a marker and she envisioned him attaching a flag to the top. When the task was complete he sat and observed it for a few moments, then selected the top stone and passed it to her. 'How many can you skim?'

Delia held the stone in her palm. It was smooth and perfect for skimming but she didn't want to throw it away into the lake.

She placed it back on top of the cairn and he reached out to straighten it.

'I know you too,' he said. 'You're that sculptor, the one who . . .'

'Whose boyfriend collapsed by the dam. Yeah, that's me.' No use pretending. 'His name was Ben. You might have seen him around.'

His face turned a little grey. 'Feel like a spliff?'

'I don't smoke.'

'A cup of tea then?'

'Okay . . . How, though, out here?'

'I've got a gas cooker.'

He stood up and walked towards a bicycle. She was surprised not to have noticed it before. A tent bag lay beside it and a few pannier bags coated in dust. The bike was claret red and flecked with rust.

She blinked a few times. Ben had owned a bike that was similar. He'd bought it in Kurow on the day they met. Her mind was becoming foggy and she shook the memory away.

'There's nothing better than sitting at a lake with a cup of tea,' Luke said.

A slight nip signalled the crisp chill of evening approaching, and she wrapped her cardigan around herself. 'Afterwards I'd better go though, or I'll be walking home in the dark.'

Luke busied himself making tea. She sat listening to the jingle and quiet clatter as he set about the task. In different circumstances he could have been Ben's brother. Their resemblance was so marked and it surprised her that this had never occurred to her before. She searched amongst the stones for a flat, rounded one. The stones, although white and pure, were easily distinguishable because of the complex web of shadows they created on one another. She picked one and turned it over in her palm. It was a perfect flat circle.

'I've heard that if a person can draw a circle they're mad,' she said, not considering that he'd listen. 'All I'd need to do is trace this.'

He looked up, the billy in his hand, and placed it on the stove, the gas hissing.

'Let's see.' He stood and walked to her, took the stone, his fingertips brushing hers. 'You're right.' He too turned it over in his palm and then motioned to throw it.

'Don't.'

'I wasn't going to.' He toyed with it, grinning. 'What do you want it for anyhow?'

Something in her chest fluttered a little, followed by a twinge of guilt. 'I could paint on it.'

Luke returned to the billy and they watched as steam emerged from the spout, rising up and mingling with the moisture in the air. He turned off the gas cooker and the hiss of gas spluttered and ceased.

'Take milk?' he asked.

'Please.'

'Powdered of course.'

He poured tea into two chipped enamel cups. They were brown and stained. He mixed a measure of powder into each of the cups and it merged with the tea, turning it opaque.

'So you'll bring it back to me then?' he asked. 'The painted stone, I mean.'

'Will you still be here?'

'I usually only stay one night.'

'Oh.'

'Sometimes longer.'

'Where do you go?'

'I'll cycle a kilometre or so and set up a new camp.' He glanced around as if anticipating his next move. 'Your tea.'

She took the chipped cup and breathed in the aroma. It was such a luxury to feel the warmth of the cup against her fingertips in the evening chill. When she'd said to Luke that she'd paint the stone, she hadn't meant it'd be for him.

'Why not just stay in the same place?' she asked.

'I like the change of scenery.'

'So if you're not going far, why do you cycle and not walk?'

'In case I want to go further.'

'There's no hurry though.'

'No, I guess not.'

'And when you run out of food you cycle back to town?'

'Yes, whatever town that may be,' he said. 'I'm on the move – for the summer at least.'

His green eyes looked kind, flecked with different shades.

'It's been a lot longer than that,' she said. 'Your father, he –'

'This is my home,' he said. 'This country, my tent. Not conventional as such but it does the trick.'

She leant forward. 'So you mean you don't have a home elsewhere?'

'One made of brick or wood?' He laughed. 'Not usually.'

Where would he get the money to live like this? It didn't make sense. A stock truck rumbled by. The scent of sheep dags and wool wafted past. She watched the truck trail into the distance, kicking up a squall of dust.

. . .

Helen sparked the ignition. She drove in the opposite direction to her daughter, Delia, so that she wouldn't be noticed. To do this she had to drive in a loop but she didn't mind. The purr of the motor jangled her nerves. People around the town had been saying there was a homeless man at the lake. The same strange young man, Luke, who had run away years ago and abandoned his father. That he lived out of a tent. She didn't believe them at first, but now here her daughter was, sitting with him. As far as Helen knew, it was the first time Delia had returned to the lake since she'd scattered Ben's ashes. Helen had done so much to protect her and she wondered if now she had to protect her from this runaway as well. She tried to think nothing of what she had seen as she drove, imagining how different things had been when Delia was little and they'd lived by the coast. Yet even then their lives had been unsure.

When she arrived home and settled onto the couch, Helen looked to the far side of the room, where staggered up the pillars of the firebox was an inlaid haphazard line of shells. Some things she'd managed to hold on to. But not many. She closed her eyes and pretended to watch the purl of the sea as it knitted whitewash over sand.

Back then, sitting on a threadbare blanket watching the water from a distance, Helen had held her daughter in her arms. The sand resisted the whitewash as the incoming tide bubbled over its surface. She'd rocked gently, singing a lullaby. She listened to the sea's murmur, and breathed in the crisp salt air. It had a slight nip to it but the sand was warm underneath her feet. The Huriawa Peninsula commanded a presence on her left; she could imagine it sucking water through its blowholes and spitting it out again. Breathing. She'd walk there if she could but her legs were tired already from carrying Delia this far. Her daughter slept, her eyelids flickering. Helen took her scarf and wrapped her in a cocoon.

A rucksack was nestled beside her; she had a few dollars in

her pocket, enough to get them to Dunedin on the Waikouaiti bus, but not sufficient to leave without a trace. If it were warmer she'd trail Delia's toes through the water, and pretend they had run away. She took a handful of sand, ran it through her fingers and repeated the motion, enjoying the texture. Once when she'd sat here a pod of orca had passed through, but today the waves hid whatever was below them, seaweed swaying at curious angles. The salt in the air cleared her airways and her thoughts.

Delia had stirred, her eyelids opening, shaded by the scarf. Helen sat her up and watched her rouse with a half-drooped expression.

'Delia,' she said to no response, 'however will we get away from here?'

She'd held her in the air and her daughter giggled, the scarf falling by her side like wings. Helen brought her back down again, placed her in the sand and watched her pick at shells.

Helen opened her eyes. The shells that lined the hearth glinted at her as if winking and the background hum of the sea seeped away. The scent of salt air lingered for a few moments. Earlier, when she'd seen Delia at the lake with the homeless man, she was certain she wouldn't interfere, but now, reminded of their past, she wasn't so sure.

. . .

Kurow sat in the shadow of the mountain cluster, the shroud of mist cutting a line between light and dark down the village centre. Greys blended into a mixture of green tinges, and shadows deepened the curves between the peaks. At the skirt of this backdrop, cottages gathered together separated only by yellowed grass and weathered fences.

Delia wandered along the street thinking how odd it was to have come across the young man who had run away. The people of Kurow and his father had mourned him, when really he can't have gone far. It was selfish of him to have left in the first place, although why he'd done it she didn't understand, or much care to. She might visit him in a few days, or maybe not. She approached her mother's house and glancing in through the window, saw her sitting on the couch, staring at the outline of the fireplace as if into nothing. When they had moved to Kurow, they'd spent an afternoon inlaying shells from Karitane up the pillar of the firebox, to remind them of the shells they had collected together and the beach, her mother had said. Delia didn't remember much of Karitane now, except the scent of salt air and falling asleep to the sound of the waves pulling and thrusting on the shore. She remembered the chill of the nights too and hiding her head beneath the cover, hiding both from the cold and arguments. She could recall her father's voice but not what he looked like. Now, as she looked in, her mother looked like a statue, locked in thoughts and time.

Delia kept walking another block and then along the footpath towards her home. The residents of Kurow mowed their lawns into tidy squares that had become parched and sparse. The taste of tea lingered in her mouth. Shadows crept over the path and she wove around them. The occasional local saw her and raised a hand or followed her movements through a windowpane. Her hair fell loose and it felt light against her cheeks.

Her cottage stood alone, cast to the side as if unwanted, and as she came closer she smiled at the familiarity of its white-painted gleam. The mountains surrounding the town hemmed it in, appearing to cut it off from the outside world. A meandering road crossing a Tee junction from her cottage's path reached out, left towards the shadows and right to the main drag. She could see a figure standing outside the cottage, her life model Jane. She liked to think of her as nameless though, simply an object. The summer evening had settled and in the fading light Delia narrowed her lids. The model knocked once and paused, knocked again, and after a few moments she turned, curvaceous against the doorframe, a surprised look passing across her face.

'Oh,' she said, 'I wondered if you weren't coming.'

Delia shook her head. 'Is it that time already? I'm so sorry, I'd forgotten.'

The model stepped away from the doorframe. 'Should we make it another time?'

'No, no, come on through.'

Delia approached the door, her hand shaking a little as she slid the key into the lock and led the way down the hall, the scent of Oamaru stone dust greeting them. Her footsteps carved a path through the layer that had settled from the studio during the day. The model followed behind.

In the studio, the model stretched her arms into the air, releasing the first garment, then bent to remove the second and the third. The piles of cotton material fell in an unkempt heap. Her naked figure changed the atmosphere in the room, the effect so stinging, it was as if someone had switched a light on. Delia watched as the model reclined on a chair without instruction, holding her posture steady with her head turned sideways but her eyes direct and forward. It must have strained her.

Delia walked away from her subject. She breathed out, running her fingertips over a row of chisels and selected one. Its blade was newly sharpened.

She returned to stand before her subject. The model's gaze was still locked, unnerving, her figure already frozen, statue-like and too confident looking.

'I'm not working on the same piece,' Delia said.

She took the model's arm and began to manoeuvre her like a mannequin. Her skin felt smooth as if coated in silk. She tilted the model's chin and gently repositioned the angle of her head, so that the direction of her stare was downwards. She stepped back to admire her subject. There was no doubt. The woman looked exquisite.

The stone fell away easily when she pounded at it, the mallet hitting the chisel. In the summer evening her skin was coated in a sheen of oil. Delia's sundress splayed around her as she moved. The hacking movements were like the dance of a conductor in time with her breath. Large chunks fell to the floor and broke apart. The dust beneath her fingernails became entrenched. The surface of it felt rough and the sound had an abstract musicality to it. The model maintained her pose. Her hazel eyes stared at an empty space on the floor, intent.

When the initial phase was complete, the stone was still rough. It had merely become a shape. Delia raised and lowered her head as she studied the model, moulding the stone with care. The frantic nature of mallet hitting chisel was now subtle, replaced by a scraping noise.

Delia continued to study the model, concentrating as she removed layers of dust with fine sandpaper. The statue was nearly complete but these fine details were important. There were soon to be two models in the room, one that was real and one that might like to be but would remain in a jail of stone.

She didn't notice when her mother entered the room but glanced up when she heard a sharp inhalation of breath.

'Oh, I'm awfully sorry.' Her mother's body tensed as she averted her eyes and stance away from the naked subject whose eyelids now opened in surprise at another entering the room.

'I keep telling you,' Delia said, 'this is art, nothing to be self-conscious about.'

Her mother continued to avert her eyes. 'Maybe not for you,' she scolded. She grabbed a nightgown perched over a chair. 'I'm sorry,' she said brusquely, 'cover up with this for a moment, will you?'

The model looked at Delia who gave a slight nod. She stood reluctant, and then with a confident flourish, wrapped the gown around herself, making certain to flash as much as she could whilst doing so. She stretched alluringly and smiled at Delia.

Delia withheld a smile. 'Mother, seriously.'

'Just a few minutes is all I need.'

She sighed, walked to the model and spoke with her, a layer of dust between them. 'I'm sorry, would you excuse us for a minute? We won't be long.'

The model nodded. 'I'll wait in the lounge. No hurry, it's okay.'

She walked gracefully from the room, her gown trailing behind her, open and exposing her nakedness. Delia knew that she'd be able to hear the entire conversation, though muffled. She thought that the model was becoming a little cocky and her mother increasingly awkward.

When the door clicked shut she turned her head. 'I'm paying her for her time, you realise.'

'I saw you at the lake.'

There was a pause as Delia registered her surprise. 'So?'

Her mother narrowed her eyes. 'People say he's homeless, and that he shouldn't be hanging around.'

'Ah, you shouldn't listen to small town gossip.'

'Do you really think it's wise spending time with him?'

Delia stared at her. 'I don't see any problem with it.' She paused, registering. 'Have you been spying on me? I only ran into him once and –'

'I just don't want to see you getting hurt.'

'Aren't I already? God, you just can't help but interfere, can you?'

Her mother paced the room, her words insistent. 'You can't just pick up where you left off and pretend nothing is the matter.'

'It's better than moping around all day.' Delia played absently with the tips of her dusty fingers, worn by the repetitive motions of her work.

'I'm only saying all this because I care about you.'

Delia's body hardened, the lines of her skin becoming lifeless like the statues around her. 'It's my life to live,' she said. 'Now if you don't mind, I'd like to get back to my work.'

Her mother stopped still though her eyes continued to pace. 'The house is full of your statues, Delia. You haven't sold one. I'm starting to think you're –'

'Enough, please!'

Silence fell between them for a few moments.

'What's going on?'

The insistence sapped at her. 'Nothing,' Delia said meekly. 'Everything is just fine now.'

She ran her hand over the head of the statue. It needed further sanding. She imagined the statue of the model listening to their conversation, opening a pair of closed eyelids and emitting a tear. Bloody nuts. She blinked the thought away, brought herself back to reality and walked to the door. 'You can come back in now.'

The model emerged and, having undoubtedly heard the conversation, her bravado seemed to have lapsed. Delia's mother was staring at her directly. The model's gown fell to the floor in a silky puddle. She assumed the same repose. Delia settled back into her work whistling to herself.

She sanded the Oamaru stone, concentrating on the curve of the model's cheek and down the length of her neck. Usually people who are naked look vulnerable, but the model didn't. Although she didn't want to, she thought of a time when she too had been vulnerable. She'd been sitting with her mother on the beach in Karitane, the salt air twisting around their ears, making hissing noises, sea spray hitting up against rocks. It was beginning to grow dim, the sun forming a semi-circle over the horizon. She'd watched her mother gather the sand in her fingers, clutching her palm to clump the sand together to form a shape with the grains. It was damp where they sat and the sand moulded easily; it clung to their clothes and skin, resembling odd shaped bruises. Her mother had dropped the sand in her palm. She'd reached her hands down and dug, pushing sand into a pile and gathering it together with the edges of her hands into a square. The top of the square she then moulded to slant downwards in the shape of a triangle. With her forefinger she carved a door and a window.

'Do you know where this is?'

'It might be our house.'

'It is.'

Her mother had drawn another window. 'And this is where you sleep, and listen to the waves.'

It wasn't usually the waves that she listened to, it was voices – her mother's, her father's, nice at first and then not. She'd watched her mother's finger continue to carve, drawing a path away from the house, continuing out and away.

'That's the road to Dunedin,' she said, 'or wherever we'd like to go.'

The sun's semi-circle was a sliver forming a spectral light over the miniature statue of their cottage. Her mother then did a peculiar thing. She picked up a shell and placed it below the window. The shell was white and delicate.

'Do you know what this is?' she asked.

'A shell outside my window.'

'No, silly,' she said, her eyes catching the last glint of the sun, 'it's a pillow.'

Delia giggled. 'Am I supposed to sleep outside?' she'd asked. 'It'll be too cold.'

Her mother took a breath, and tilted her head as if someone might be listening. 'It's so that tonight, when you crawl out of your window, you'll have somewhere soft to land.'

Delia stared at her, feeling inquisitive, as if a game were about to begin.

Her mother lowered her eyes back to the sand where the outline of the path had now faded. She drew her finger once more slowly along it. 'And then we'll follow this path,' she said.

The chill gathered around them, and Delia felt afraid.

'Delia, are you okay?'

She looked up to see the model had put her gown back on and seated herself.

'I must be just a little tired,' Delia said.

Her hand had fallen limp and the sand paper was on the floor of the studio by her feet.

'Who was your mother talking about, at the lake?'

'No one. Just a traveller I was keeping company for a while.'

Her mother was worried about nothing. Luke was just a speck in a wide space, and she'd almost forgotten him.

. . .

Leaving Delia's studio, Helen sat in her car for a few minutes. She traced her finger over the steering wheel. The air inside the car was trapped and humid and the steering wheel warm to touch. She gazed out of the car window along the path leading to Delia's cottage. She watched a trail of dust emerge from the studio window and noticed that her daughter's tapping had become more aggressive – a cathartic drum with her chisel. It reminded her of the repeated thrum of waves pulling whitewash over sand and stone. She sat in her car for a long time, and after a while she saw Jane, Delia's model emerge. The woman was walking swiftly but when Helen opened her car door the model turned her head.

'Jane,' Helen called. 'I need to talk with you.'

Jane looked perplexed to see her again but walked towards her. Helen stepped out of her car.

'There's something I have to tell you . . . about Delia.'

Jane furrowed her brows.

'Have you heard about Ben? And what happened?'

'Some. There aren't any secrets around here.'

'No, I guess not.'

After Jane left, Helen returned to her car. Jane had said that Delia didn't talk with her about anything much, but that might change. It wasn't right to spy on her daughter but it seemed the only one way to keep her safe. A droplet carved a path along her cheek and met with the corner of her mouth. She parted her lips and the tear caught on her tongue. The taste lingered. Hurriedly, she wiped her cheek. Sun shimmied in through the window and reflected off the cottage's white weatherboard; it was too bright. She shaded her eyes and sparked the ignition.

Helen parked close to the Benmore Dam. She closed the car door behind her and made her way through a raggedy selection of rocks to where a weeping willow dipped its limbs to sway. The hem of the mountains formed shadows over the lake, dividing the water into blue and lead grey. Here it was shaded. A cairn of stones had been built, and beside it shells gathered together too, so that she could just make out Ben's name, spelt in full, the lettering skewed by the wind. Delia had placed flowers, but these were dried now and looked weary beside the cairn.

She remembered the dust Delia had dispersed with Ben's ashes, tinting the lake a troubled slate before seeping under its surface. The dust wasn't like the off-white stone dust that coated the floor in her daughter's studio, beneath the Oamaru stone chunks she sculpted with — it was darker, charred. Delia had cast it out in handfuls, and although there hadn't been a wisp of wind that day, each grain had been reluctant to fall. It had hung for a moment before descending downwards and sideways, spreading out and around. Helen hadn't wanted to intrude but couldn't cope with being far from her daughter either. When Delia finally turned, her face was pale and blank and her cheeks dry. Since that day, she and her daughter had not been close, as day by day, Delia pushed her away. And the more she'd tried to care for her, the further Delia turned.

It was clear Delia hadn't been here for some time, had possibly not returned since. Her daughter had always been fiercely independent and in many ways reminded Helen of herself. She too didn't seek help when she needed it most. The weeping willow swayed, the reflected movements dizzying below the translucent surface of the lake. Helen repositioned the shells to recreate his name.

∫∫∫

She tucked Delia into bed, whispering to her that she'd hear a tap on her window when it was time. Listening as the waves brushed onto the shore, caressing the sand and half-broken shells, she looked out from her window; the sky was too bright, the daylight reluctant to farewell the village.

She perched on a chair at the kitchen bench and blocked out the sound of the waves to listen to him breathing. Her husband was slumped on the couch, the cotton strands beneath him worn. An empty glass had fallen sideways at his feet, and a dribble of whiskey trickled onto the carpet. A familiar scent enveloped the room, salt air struggling to pierce through alcohol. She looked at his face. It was covered in an oily sheen as if strained. He appeared dead, his skin sullen, his features unmoving, and were it not for the rattle of air that emerged from his lips, she might have imagined him so.

Helen waited, and as his breathing became deeper, she stood, took a blanket from the side of the couch and covered him. His head was tilted backwards at a low ceiling, towards nothing. He wasn't cruel, had never been so, but looking at him now she felt little sadness. He wasn't enough, couldn't give her or Delia enough. The smell of whiskey rose. She turned, her stomach nauseated.

Her footsteps were quiet across the floorboards but he wouldn't have heard her anyhow even if she'd been stomping. She went to the door and opened it, stepped through, and clicked it shut. The trees around her didn't stir and she felt exposed under

25

the silvery purple shimmer of the moon. She went to the garage and collected a backpack and a pillow. The salt air filled her lungs; her movements swift.

The window where Delia lay was slightly ajar. She tapped on it gently and held the pillow in her arms, outstretched, the pillow resembling a cloud awaiting the girl's fall. Delia's face appeared quickly; she mustn't have been asleep. It reflected off-white through the glass, like an apparition. She didn't smile. Her fingers pushed at the window, leaving a handprint of smudges, and then she clasped onto the sill and clambered out. The action was well practised, she was like one adept at clambering in trees. Her weight was cushioned by the feathers beneath the cotton, and as Helen carried her, the waves seemingly became louder to mask their disappearance.

To her alarm, Delia began to whisper. 'Don't carry me,' she said, her words quieter than the rustle of trees. 'I can walk on my own.'

Helen smiled and placed her daughter on the grass beside the path, looking back once at the cottage by the sea, the one that was supposed to have been perfect. Then she turned to see that Delia was already leading the way, her footsteps making a path towards the gate.

∫∫∫

Delia sat nestled in the grass in front of her cottage, surrounded by tubes of paint and a bowl of turpentine. She held in her hand a fine paintbrush and a flat water-worn stone. It had been a few days and she still hadn't returned to visit Luke. He'd probably have moved on again by now. She placed the stone on her knee, looking at it intently, the paintbrush poised. Her fingers shook a little.

The stone was lightly warmed by the sun and felt steady on her skin. It was aged. She felt like a thief. Perhaps she should by the dark of the night return to the lake and give back the stone to its rightful home. Who was she to assume that by painting it she was giving it some greater purpose? In a moment of madness she'd offered to paint a rock as a gift. Now, in retrospect, this seemed lame, but she'd resolved to try anyway. She hovered the paintbrush above the stone and mimicked how she might begin. The lake a combination of blues, shadowed and deep; two figures stooped over a billy beside a tent; a single distant hawk receding into a pale sky. Shit, this is going to be difficult. How might it be possible to fit this scene into such a confined space?

She took a sip of tea and picked up a tube of paint. The tea she'd made with powdered milk so that her memories of the scene might be triggered. As she began to paint, her eyes blurred; the image in her mind started to change and rearrange. The tent collapsed, the hawk was obscured and the sky became winter bright. A memory of Ben at the Manorburn Dam crept over the stone's surface. The Dam had frozen over. Stooping to a billy, Ben picked it up and poured water over glowing embers. Accompanied by an angry sizzle, the glow changed from amber to charcoal. Ice crackled as curlers hefted their stones. At the side of the Dam, chatter of tourists and locals rattled in her ears. They lined up beside a caravan to rent ice skates. She saw in the scene that she had pulled her skates on, was smiling and had cast off, dodging children swinging in pirouettes. Ben had his skates on too, edged his way to the ice and stood up, wobbling slightly. He'd propelled himself forward unsteadily and was making a semicircle towards her, then he caught her by the tips of her fingers and swung away. He drew her in close to him to dance. His face was clear for a moment. His eyes smiling. The little lines that framed them curling. Then as quickly as the memory arrived he faded, as if a layer of ice had crackled up between them and she was swept away. She saw the pair of them, their bodies frozen in a waltz in a painting on a stone.

Disappointed, she realised she was back to her spot in the grass, alone beside her cottage in Kurow. The noise around her was now subtle and the air warm. Her hunched figure surrounded by mixed paints, newspaper, a bowl of dirty turps, and an empty enamel cup. The memory lasted only a few seconds and yet the painting on the stone in her hand was finished. She held it close, then far away, and saw the lines and hues of the scene weren't accurate. It was impossible to capture. She felt nauseous. The image she'd painted wasn't the lakeside with Luke, not as she'd intended.

She thrust the stone into the bowl of turps and rubbed the image off. Tomorrow she'd try again. She would paint the campsite and the lake and return the stone to Luke. If he was still there. By seeing Luke she would try to stop thinking of Ben, and what he had done. Standing by the lake amongst the pylons, skimming stones and watching the shimmer of the surface as each stone fell, she'd seen them, Ben and the model across the other side. Her stomach turned.

That following evening as she returned to her cottage, walking gingerly on bare feet across the grass, she carried the newly painted stone, clamped between her thumb and forefinger so as not to smudge it. As she walked she saw that the sky had darkened, turning her cottage's white cladding a dull grey accompanied by a chill. Kurow was split in two as evening set, half in shadow and half out. The cottage would be perfect, if only she could manoeuvre it to where the sun wasn't so easily waylaid by the mountains. The wisteria wrapping around it, so quaint in the sunshine, acquired a murky personality and began to clench and trap her inside.

Come nightfall, she looked out between the window frames, and through the wisteria that snuck at their edges. Paints and utensils strewn in the grass, brushes rinsed but knocked out of their jar, pointing in the direction of Aviemore. The expanse above was inky and clear. In the direction she locked her gaze, but far enough that she couldn't see, Luke's khaki tent had been erected for the night.

2

In the fading light Luke took his fishing rod and laid it flat by the water's edge. His stomach rumbled. He walked away from the campsite, closer to the roadside where a row of poplars swayed. His fingers tossed aside the larger rocks. He picked one up in each hand and gouged at the dirt. It stung underneath his nails, and the exertion coated his forehead with a sheen of sweat. A tail flickered just beyond his grasp. Its body glistened and then vanished. He dug deeper and, with his thumb and forefinger, pulled a worm from its escape. He squeezed and it died instantly. He pulled a second and it too hung lifeless in his fingers. The first worm he brushed off and swallowed, then attached the second to a hook and cast out the line into the evening light. No food was wasted, not even the most disgusting. He was used to it and didn't retch.

The smell of searing trout wafted across the campsite. Luke chewed on strips of flesh. Afterwards he buried the bones at the spot where he'd dug the worms.

He felt around inside his tent for the jersey he kept beside his mat and a baggy hat to rest askew on his head, put his feet into a pair of gumboots, sat on a rock and watched his breath rise. The lake stretched before him, a burnish of silver gracing its surface. Two ghosts danced pirouettes on it. He shook his head to shake the image away but the ghosts remained.

He watched them, smiling to tempt their friendship. Each figure was blurred, lingering somewhere between life and death. The man had bare feet and looked weatherworn and free. The woman turned her head, acknowledging Luke's figure perched in the darkness. Two sharp eyes stared at him. Startled, he realised the apparition looked just like Delia. This jarred him. Since he'd met her by the side of the lake, she hadn't returned, and he was starting to wonder whether she'd ever visited him at all. His eyes and mind fell heavy. The ghosts with their piercing eyes waltzed a slow diagonal in one direction and then the other, criss-crossing the corners of his skull until they faded from his sight. She may have turned to farewell him, her sundress swirling in the night, but he couldn't be sure. Too much time alone; he must be losing it. When he looked up again, he saw what he had thought to be figures were worn down pylons — like those that once must have held up a jetty, and that the shapes of the pylons had warped with the lull of the lake into contours. He returned to his tent. The isolation of the landscape covered him in a blanket and he fell asleep.

The first breath of the morning painted a spreading stroke of light and colours expanding across the hills. Luke slept through, stepping out from his tent when the sun was bright. The lake beckoned him. He removed his clothes, revealing a sinewy body, and dived beneath the water's depths. Reborn and shivering, he set about his morning routine and when this was done, he sat with a cup of tea facing the lake. If the apparitions danced then they did so invisibly and in secret. They may have retired for the day to sleep, curled up somewhere in the privacy of a tree shadow.

Late morning, Luke heard the crunch of stones. Delia appeared beside him, a smile lurking at the corners of her mouth. She wasn't an apparition after all.

'Are you moving on?' she asked.

'Delia,' he exclaimed.

She shuffled a little. 'Painting this was harder than I expected.'

He noticed her hand searching in her pocket and she handed the stone to him, watching his reaction. The stone lay flat in his palm, the painting on its surface so finely rendered the brush strokes couldn't be seen.

'Oh,' he said, 'you're good.'

'Don't sound too surprised.'

'You captured it.'

'Not in one try.'

'Is it for me?'

She nodded.

'I'll keep it with me wherever I go.'

'Won't it weigh down your pack?'

'I don't care.'

'Well, at least you'll carry one material possession with you.'

'Sure,' he smiled, 'I will.'

The scene she'd painted gave his campsite a permanence in his life that he was unfamiliar with. Silty stones layering the base of the lake remained untouched and so, too, did those beneath the hardened skin of his feet. The stone he held, carefully selected. He studied it in appreciation for a few moments and then turned his attention to her. It wasn't cold but he shivered.

He watched her settle amongst the stones and remove her backpack. It bulged.

'I've brought you some food,' she said, beginning to unzip the pack. She shook off her jandals, smiling.

'I was going to cycle back to town soon,' he said, ill at ease. 'You're too generous.'

She removed a pile of supplies from the pack and with a flourish pulled out a packet of tea bags.

'You didn't have to.'

'Yes, I did,' she said. 'And besides, they're not all for you.' She was grinning.

'You can't go dishing out groceries to just anyone, you know.'

She looked at the foodstuffs piled on the rocks. 'You earn nothing though. I wanted to help.' Her cheeks flushed.

'Delia . . .' He paused. 'Maybe I won Lotto.'

She shook her head. A silence stretched.

The cairn had tumbled into disarray and she picked up a couple of stones and attempted to fix it, layering a variety of rocks into a precarious pile. She looked up for a moment before placing the final stone. Two brown curls fell down either side of her face, framing her as if she were staring at him between a set of misshapen curtains. Something about her seemed to be haphazard, and this appealed to him.

He took the painted stone and placed it on top, stepped back, then turned his head aside and scanned the lake. An iridescent hue merged into depths of teal, a slight wind graced its surface.

It was time for him to move on. He stood up and began to remove the ropes that secured his tent. 'Wanna help?' he asked her.

She nodded and they set about pulling at poles and pegs. The tent breathed out a sigh and collapsed. She helped him roll it into a leather satchel, and stood beside him. He skipped a rock across the lake's surface.

'Where will you camp next?'

'I don't know,' he said. 'But it won't be far.'

'You know, since you've won the lottery you could live anywhere – in a house, I mean.'

He sighed and lowered his head. 'I'm not ready for that.'

'So what will you do?' she asked.

'This.'

'Just this?'

'Yes.'

'You mean look out at lakes and mountains until you're an old man?'

'I don't know.' He hung his head. 'I'm not sure what my purpose is. It's selfish, isn't it?'

'How so?'

'I'm never going to work another day in my life. I'm spending all of the Lotto money on myself.'

Her expression was confused.

'I'll leave only marks in the soil.'

'It isn't enough,' she said, resolute. 'There is more to life than just watching it.'

'I'm not sure,' he said. 'To me, being lost is enough, and being free to do as I please.'

She looked at him, her face blank. 'I'd better go,' she said. 'It's time you set up a new camp.'

He nodded. 'I'll ride you to the roadside if you like?' He pulled his bike from the grass.

She smiled and climbed onto the back of it, her sundress trailing behind her. Her figure was slight but he wobbled and righted himself as he set off. His bike parted the stones easily, carving a path away.

Luke set up his new camp, pausing to watch as cirrus clouds played in the sky, fresh brushstrokes of white widening the horizon. The lake too was swollen, not by rainfall, but by the fusion of its colour. A single hawk passed above casting a shadow over the water.

When evening fell, the concrete tone of the sky and chill in the air mixed with his mood. Delia was gone again and he didn't know if she'd return. He would remain alone, moving from one campsite to another until he was too old to pedal.

For the first time he wondered if his choices in life were right or whether he was simply a fool with no shoes.

Luke had moved his camp site three times. The heat of each day was jarring and he sought shaded spots to hide his tent from the sun's shards. As he took pegs from their cotton sack they clanged against each other, making him shiver. One after the other he burrowed their tips into the crusted dirt. Their rounded hooks left red indents in his skin. He persevered, heaving. 'For fuck's sake,' he said, rubbing his sore palms together. Nobody heard him. At the bottom of the peg bag he pulled out one final object, the painted stone. On each occasion he'd moved, he'd been sure to remember to bring it with him. He put it into his pocket. When he finished erecting the tent and his gear was inside, he placed the stone underneath his pillow.

His skin singed and complained. The tent was hotter inside than outside, but at least hid him from the sun's harshest glare. He lay naked on top of his sleeping bag, welcoming thin streams of lake air through the tent door. When he pulled himself up to fill a battered stainless steel bottle in the lake, his body felt heavy and reluctant, the sun creating a shimmer over his treacly skin.

Eventually night fell, bringing with it a mild cooling. He unzipped his sleeping bag, tucked himself into it, reading under the dull sheen of light that pressed through nylon.

After a time he became weary and placed the book beneath his pillow, his hand brushing up against the painted stone. He closed his eyes; beneath his lids and in a half-baked dream Delia unzipped the door, arriving sheepish and smiling. Bloody stupid, he thought, thinking of a stranger like this.

The mild air became a cocoon, surrounding and protecting them. Despite the warmth, she was shivering. She removed her clothes without a shadow of self-consciousness, unzipped the sleeping bag wide and crawled to lay beside him. Her body was long and sleek. She felt real.

His head clouded and his body tensed. He sat up in the tent, shaking his thoughts away. What was he doing thinking of Delia? He didn't even know her. Not really. He knew a lot about her. That she'd moved from Dunedin with her mother. He knew her boyfriend had died suddenly. Maybe from a heart attack or a brain aneurism or something like that, he wasn't exactly sure. Luke had gone to school with Ben, but he didn't know him, not well anyway. He was the sort of guy who had been confident in school, a couple of years older. Anyhow, people in small towns talk and . . . well, he'd felt sorry for Delia before he left. Really bloody sorry for her. But, with a life on the move he'd try to be careful not to get too close to her.

It had been a few days though since she had visited him and he resolved to visit her at least, wherever she might be. He'd knock on every door in Kurow if he had to. All twenty.

3

During the day, as Delia wiled away the hours sculpting, the sun baked the earth in and around her cottage. The air felt hazy with heat, confused almost. Kurow had started to become dehydrated, the squares of yellowed grass marking its edges becoming hems surrounding glazed earth. The mountains were changing in colour, a mixture of ochre and shadow. Delia was relieved when darkness fell, taking with it the dry heat and covering her in welcome seclusion. From her window she saw the lights of the township turn out, could all but hear each light switch click.

She waited.

Then she opened a door, her dress trailing behind her, touched a lamp on and perched herself in an armchair, its cover worn. She took a shawl from its arm and wrapped it around her. The lamp's circumference was made of paper and through it light escaped, making shadows and shimmers in the far corners, layering the room with a sad overtone, as if trying to cover hidden secrets tucked into the pages of brown, aged novels. She inhaled a long breath and looked around at the white stucco walls lined with artists' books, novels, statues of Ben that were failures – and memories.

The statues, like her mind, were full of secrets. Some stared intently while others cried baubles of dust, their eyes blurry and worried – the irises containing no colour; their stony hearts no beat. She no longer felt content here. Words in the novels that had once contained new pathways and trails of thought no longer offered comfort from all that distracted and disturbed her.

She stirred, becoming aware of her body encased in the armchair. Each night she sat in this room; the routine had become her refuge. Sleep was reluctant to claim her but when it finally did wish to visit she didn't let it. There was something strangely comforting in the fact that whilst others slept she did not. Her body was deprived and hungry for rest but her thoughts swam in many directions, awakened as if it were not night.

She sat upright in her armchair, returning the stare of a statue she considered her closest likeness to Ben, or at least a shell of him. She had repeatedly tried to capture something that he had exuded but could not. There was more to it than that though, by sculpting Ben, she was able to recreate the version of him that she had known before seeing him at the lakeside with Jane. The light from the lamp shaped eerie shadows on the statue, accentuating its eyes and features.

In Delia's imagination, the statue gave the impression of being only dimly aware of her presence. Its eyes looked at her, beyond her and through her. Besides the statues, the room was kept as Ben had left it. They'd only lived together for a year or so but had in that time been inseparable, or so she'd thought. He had placed the books on the shelves in alphabetical order, an act she'd thought quirky and endearing, he'd been so dishevelled in other ways. They stood still as a tribute to this task, not to be disturbed. She had, though, hoarded statues, cluttering the room into claustrophobic disarray and layering the carpet with off-white dust coloured like the stones lining the lake at Aviemore.

She visualised her day at the lake and her nervous hands

shivering as she had tried to reconstruct the cairn. The air between her and the statue began to change and swirl. Memories clouded her thoughts.

'Are you coming home tomorrow?' she mouthed.

There was silence. She thought of Ben and how he had lain by the roadside. His face pale and still, powdery looking almost, as if he might dissolve like powdered milk into tea. How she couldn't breathe. And then in the days after how she hadn't been able to move, or grieve, or try to be herself ever again; how she existed in limbo wanting to retrieve the essence of something she no longer could. On the day, he'd gone out for a bit, a walk maybe, or some sort of errand, she couldn't recall. And, after a while, when he hadn't returned, she'd gone to find him, thinking to pick him up and go somewhere. Anywhere, it hadn't mattered.

When the statue in front of her didn't reply she pleaded with the others, asking each one the same desperate question. The lack of response gnawed at her insides. She felt dry and depleted.

She ran her fingertips over the statue's cheek. It didn't soften. She waited for the statue to return her thoughts. The stone remained empty. A solitary tear carved its way down her cheek. The statue was simply dormant, and she would wait for it to awaken. She wondered how many more nights she would have to wait, alone and swallowed by shadows.

'Could I rename you Luke?' she asked playfully. 'That wouldn't be so hard now, would it?'

She leant forward a little towards the statue of Ben.

Another tear followed the first and she closed her weary eyes. She curled into the armchair, resisting sleep. The statues gathered her into an embrace and she finally succumbed.

She dreamt of the lakeside and a jumbled collage of images. The outline of a khaki tent, a chipped claret-red bicycle, milk powder falling like snow and mingling with the lake, turning it off-white. She dreamt she was swimming, the cloudy water surrounding her, warm and thick, becoming one with a sky of white sheets and devouring her. The white substance swallowed the khaki tent too, and when it receded the tent was gone, leaving her alone.

At some point during the early morning she arose, bereft and dazed. The statues watched her leave and speckles of dust followed her.

. . .

Luke's bike meandered forward. Its movement was creaky from exposure to the elements. A thin veil of sweat clung to his skin and cooled him as the air swam over and past. He rode away from the lake, leaving his tent and belongings vulnerable to passers-by. Then over the Dam, his body a stickman above a large expanse of water. Delia, he knew, must live in Kurow.

As he cycled into town he scanned each house he passed and sought her whereabouts at the local petrol station. He recognised a wizened local who pointed him in the direction of a cottage not so far from the centre of town.

Approaching, he felt intrusive. Maybe she hadn't returned to the lake for a reason; he should respect her rejection and continue on his journey as if they had never met.

The cottage was quaint. He spied the outline of a statue through a window, the silhouette of a naked woman. Perhaps the statue, like the apparition a few nights ago, might turn and greet him. He longed to be welcomed inside.

A shadow passed across the curtain and he saw Delia wander through the room, then turn. It felt strange to glimpse her in an environment beyond the lake and he felt a pinch of nerves.

He laid his bike on the ground. The grass was long and untended and the bike became easily hidden amongst it. Walking up the driveway, the door opened before he was able to knock and Delia stood in the doorway.

'Hello,' she said. 'I thought you might come.'

'Did you?'

'I've been waiting for you.'

She ushered him inside and closed the door behind him. It clicked. He wasn't used to feeling enclosed. He wondered if she sensed his uncertainty as she guided him through the dim hallway and into a lounge. The room was lined with smiling statues welcoming him.

'I'm glad to meet your statues,' he said.

She looked at them as if they were new acquaintances.

'They're not self-portraits,' he murmured.

'No, indeed.'

He realised that she looked drawn. Her eyes had lost their reflective shimmer and the skin beneath had darkened. She looked slim compared to the healthy full statues around her. She must have been working hard, chiselling and sanding, so maybe that was why she hadn't returned to visit him lately.

'I'll show you my studio,' she said.

The studio was brighter than the other parts of the house. Light flowing freely from wide windows contrasted starkly with the dim hallway and lounge. Although aerated, the room was filled with a lingering powdery scent. He felt both absorbed and disturbed by it. Antique tools hung from hooks, and statues in various stages of production lined the room. He felt in the presence of an audience that was assessing him. She stood before

41

him, her head raised, her eyes smiling but her face still.

She gestured towards a block of stone. A large chisel and mallet lay on it. 'I've saved this one for you.'

She took his hand and guided him to pose before the stone. A current of warmth coursed through him.

'I want you to imagine you're at the lake,' she said. 'I want you to lose yourself in that.'

He nodded and shyly positioned himself on the floor, tried to imagine a layer of stones supporting him, and below that the crust of another unknown layer. Attempting to banish the lingering powdery taste that came from the statues nearby, he inhaled a fresh breath, feeling the lake coursing and gyrating as if angry at him, and closed his eyes.

Delia lowered the chisel to the stone.

There came a time, on Delia's dusty floor, when Luke felt his skin becoming rubbed raw and detached. The statue she was making could never be right. It wasn't that she didn't have ability, but he was always on the move and this statue couldn't. He felt trapped now as if he too were locked in stone.

'I'm tired,' he said.

He stretched his stiffened limbs and moved to stand beside the gaping window. The fresh air smelt of freedom. He breathed it in until it circulated all of his veins and muscles.

Delia lowered her mallet though her knuckles tightened around the handle of the chisel. 'I'm sorry, sometimes time just runs away and you looked so relaxed.'

'I was, I suppose, to begin with.'

'It's painful isn't it?'

'Yes.'

'Staying put, I mean.'

He nodded, surprised at her understanding. His bike glinted at him from amidst a layer of grass. Delia moved to stand beside him, wrapped her fingers into his – intertwining them, creating a lock.

'You can't stay here, can you?' she said.

He felt the walls caving in on him, dust suffocating him, making him think of the claustrophobia of his childhood, surrounded by rows of cherry trees – an orchard he could not escape. She was staring at him, as if expectant.

'No.'

She sighed and moved away. He thought of his tent waiting for him, the crawling nights he'd spent. 'You'll come with me,' he said.

He couldn't help but think she looked a little afraid.

'Not just yet,' she said.

She reached up to his cheek. Her fingers were shaking. She trailed her fingertips down his neck and then down further still.

He drifted with her touch.

∫∫∫

On the outskirts of Kurow, close to the Aviemore Dam and submerged in the baked furrows of a cherry orchard, Luke sat. His shoes were strewn and his feet bare, coated in fine dust. The piercing sun attempted to segue through the lush leaves, splattering him in misshapen chequers of light. Surrounding him were recently discarded pips of cherries, fringed with red flesh. He had never grown tired of the taste. An empty cherry bucket lay on its side, beckoning to be filled. His hands were stained red, evidence of buckets he'd filled on other days.

In his hand he held his favourite book, its cover faded by the sun, smudged red in places and held together with tape. He'd found it in the attic but it now sat as part of a meagre collection in his bedroom. Whenever an opportunity arose he snuck here, to this spot beneath the shade of the trees, with one of his books tucked under his arm. He could find this spot easily, even if he were blind.

Luke was immersed in the book, its curious mixture of words offering an escape. In the story he read of a young nomad who had run away from home. He thought that if his father came lumbering through the trees to find him, perhaps he'd be able to hide behind the leaves long enough for the sun to sink. Start a new life living in the trees, moving from one spot to the next each evening, eating cherries and sucking rainwater from leaves and roots. He shivered. Each hour he spent here was another two buckets he was supposed to have filled, but the words of the book were too moreish to put down and every cherry picked too monotonous to bear.

'Luke,' he heard his father call.

The voice reverberated around the orchard and back through his veins, yet he remained silent.

He reluctantly folded the page into a triangle to mark his place. The nomad would need to seek adventure on his own for another few hours. The voice called again, creating a wind that whipped up the leaves, dust and grass that surrounded him. The wind escalated into a tornado, sucking him upwards into the tree. He hugged the trunk and held tightly to his book, trying to become the same colour as the bark – the way a skink latches onto schist. His skin, bones and blood mimicked its texture. The tornado didn't let up. It pressed his body against the trunk. His heart pounded and his veins joined with the sap running through the tree and breathed with it all in one continuous motion, roots to tip. He scrambled up.

From the relative safety of the treetop he viewed the empty bucket on the ground. It glowed bright. He had to retrieve it or be doomed. He lowered himself to a branch and his camouflage began to subside. The skink resembled a boy once more.

Visible. Vulnerable.

He clambered down, each crunch and snapped twig ringing terror in his ears and body. His fingers became slippery with nerves and he lost hold of his book. He watched as it collided with the ground, scattering its pages. He continued his descent. The tornado had stopped but Luke's fear remained.

He took hold of the bucket. It gleamed and called loudly to its master. He heard his father thudding through the trees, gumboots clomping. A broad shadow hovered over him, dwarfing him. It stretched its tendrils, doubling in size. He tried to turn back into a skink and mould himself into the hardened earth. He looked up to see his father frowning into the empty bucket.

'C'mon, there's work to be done.' Spittle emerged as he spoke. 'We don't have time for this.'

The book lay askew in the grass, its entrails scattered in a semi-circle around the trunk. His father's calloused hand clenched around his arm and carted him between the trees, where closer at hand to his father's watchful eye, he was set to work. Like his book, Luke was torn. He picked cherries with a blank face. The nomad's journey had ended.

That night a wind emerged and the beloved pages of the nomad book scattered further. Some clung to branches, others to furrows. He crept from his bedroom window into the dark. His hand clutched a torch but didn't switch it on until the orchard enveloped him. The trees became threatening in the gloom, brushing at him and mocking him. The scanty beam of the torch offered little reassurance. He followed the black outlines of the trees through the maze and located the spot where his book had been scattered. Silvery slithers of the moon, reflecting a sun far away, illuminated an odd assortment of pages. He set about collecting these, gathering them under the crook of his arm. He used the torch to search amidst branches and grass. His hands brushed off dust and continued to forage. He took his time and each page collected soothed his anxiety.

His body became drowsy so he returned through the maze and climbed in through his bedroom window. He laid the pages around him. Some were crumpled and mildly damaged but all were salvageable. He placed each page carefully into the correct order. His eyes started to droop and sleep begged at the corners of his consciousness. He rubbed his eyelids and forced the longing away. Instead he found the page folded at its corner and continued to read. As he read the last page his zest faded. The watery gloss that covered his eyes gathered into a droplet. Somewhere in the orchard, fluttering beyond his grasp, were the final few pages of the novel. He knew the ending so well but now the book didn't know it, and couldn't tell it to him again. The fate of the nomad was his to decide.

∫∫∫

Delia opened her eyes. She had fallen asleep, and when she awoke was surprised to see that Luke remained beside her. His body was slumped with his hand resting by his face, coated in Oamaru stone powder. The ground beneath him was hard and cold and the dust that coated him made him appear ghostly. He had come to her studio, been sculpted and then lain on the floor as if deceased.

She felt an overwhelming wave of guilt. Was it Ben who lay on the floor or Luke? His face was pale and still, like Ben's had been by the roadside, powdery looking as if he might dissolve. Her breathe caught in her throat. She didn't know if she'd indulged herself because of their similarity or as a feeble attempt to move on.

Delia propped herself up a little and leant over Luke. He didn't stir. He had joined the statues and became an object she could imprint. A second passing of guilt wafted through her. The curve of his shoulder was olive. She could reach out and touch him. His eyelashes were still. If she were sleeping, would he study her too? He wouldn't. She thrummed her fingers across her thigh and wondered why he might be on the run.

As she stood and walked away, her feet created footprints in the dust. She left the door ajar and went to her bedroom. The air was lighter there – unladen with dust – and warm. She switched on a light and looked at herself in the mirror above her dresser. Her hair was scraggly and her cheeks smudged white. She brushed her hands over her face as if washing it, closing her eyes. When she opened them again a face stared back at her that wasn't hers. Her eyes had blurred and she wiped them clear, revealing darker skin, piercing eyes, shoulder blades that were curved and elegant and a woman's body that wasn't hers. She was too shocked to gasp and turned away from the reflection of the model – Jane, chastising her mind, banishing her thoughts. The image in the mirror haunted her just like Luke's still figure in the dust. She tried to calm herself, to quieten the beating of her heart.

She hurriedly collected a bag of belongings. Not many. Whatever she could find that was nearby. A window was ajar and she attempted to close it. Wisteria had gathered at its edge and she pushed it outside, breaking the pieces that were pressing in. In the looming darkness she didn't like that the window framed an empty street that was shadowed by hills, where people hid behind closed doors. She averted her eyes from the window and from the mirror. The bag filled, she stood at her doorway as shadows fell around her. Her duvet was pulled back and she looked at the imprint of where she lay each night. Here in a cottage that was all she had, alone.

She turned to see Luke in the hallway. He simply stood there, smiling, as if he were still in sleep but had walked to see her.

'Are you ready to go?' she asked.

Her voice was airy, as if unconnected to herself. *Ready to go?* She wasn't ready to go anywhere, not with someone who wasn't Ben. When she looked at Luke though, his smile was reassuring and something in her became lighter. She felt protective of him. A flutter of excitement at the unknown. She hoped the mirror reflection had changed, and to check, she wiped her cheek, then held her hand in front of her. The palm was covered in dust.

She was herself again. Delia.

'Yup,' he said. His face was blank. 'If you have any food we could take that. Keep us going for a few days.'

She nodded and led him away.

In the bedroom, twigs of broken wisteria had fallen through the window frame to the carpet. The mirror reflected an empty surface of shiny silver and shadow.

• • •

Luke helped Delia collect food from the kitchen. Stuff that could last without being in a fridge. Travelling by bicycle, they could only carry so much. He filled a second hessian bag and pulled it over his shoulder, walking to the door. She followed him like a shadow that had detached itself but couldn't stay far away. The evening was quickly becoming dim and the leaves stirred. A light wind brushed dust off him, flaking powdery white shapes downwards in no hurry.

It was unusual to have another person astride the bicycle, not to mention their bags of groceries, and it was difficult for him to sit comfortably. Delia perched on the handlebars, clinging tightly with the hessian bags dangling from her arms. It would have made sense for her to have brought a backpack but neither of them had thought about that at the time. A pair of curtains closed as they cycled by and a retired car glinted metallic grey, surrounded by overgrown grass. There was a watery scent to the air, and as if by autopilot he carved their way to the lake. The road with Delia accompanying him seemed shorter than he remembered. Yet with her blocking the breeze he was warmer than usual.

. . .

Pale water lapping at the stones by her feet, Delia watched Luke lower a trout over an open flame. The fire blackened its skin from opal-green. His figure was hunched over the task, as if he'd forgotten she was there.

Knowing he wasn't watching her, she picked up the milk powder tin and prised it open. It made a subtle squeak and a puff of powder emerged. She stifled a cough. A waft of the searing trout tainted the air. Carefully she turned the tin on its side and poured some powder onto her palm. A little escaped and fell between her fingers onto the stones.

She waded a few steps into the water so that her ankles were covered, and even though it was summer, her feet instantly felt chilled. A leaf floated by, turned ginger brown. She cast the milk powder out in a handful, tinting the lake a troubled slate before it seeped below its surface. Only a little residue remained, stuck with perspiration to the lines on her hands that resembled tree roots. She cast again, and the powder hung for a moment before being flung downwards and sideways.

She remembered her mother sitting behind her when she had dispersed Ben's ashes, like she was pretending to do with the milk powder now. How she had wanted so much to curl into her arms that day and hadn't. Since then she'd become less and less close to her mother, pushing her away. Delia turned, only to find the space behind her wasn't as she recalled. It was empty.

'Are you hungry?' Luke asked without looking up.

She wasn't, but knew she should be. 'A bit.'

Wading further into the water, she let it submerge her lower legs. She reached into the water and foraged with her feet for shells. They were sharp and mostly in fragments so she searched for whole ones. The water was clear. She used the shells to spell out three letters that blurred with the movement of the lake.

A reflection hovered over its surface and her hand shook beneath the water. She dropped the last part of the letter in fright – a half-shell to complete the N.

'The trout's cooked.'

She turned and Luke's face met hers, almost identical to Ben's reflection except not skewed or blurred.

'What are you up to anyhow?'

'It's nothing,' she said, running her hand over the shells to muddle them.

Thankfully the milk powder had seeped below the surface and he didn't notice it. The memories of Ben haunting her fell away as she looked at Luke and he took her hand. Droplets fell as he did so but otherwise her palm was empty.

'Something the matter?' he asked.

'No, everything's just fine.'

He was looking at her as if confused.

That night, Delia sat in Luke's tent as the darkness gathered around them. The tent's walls glowed. A steadily depleting hessian bag of food lay beside them, and their bellies were full and content. Piles of stones held in place each corner of the tent. Her life in her cottage was far away and for now, forgotten.

She heard a click. Luke was hanging a lantern from a hook above. Looking at him, she sighed; dust had followed him from her cottage, whitening the outline of his face, like when Ben used to return from a day at work covered in chimney dust. Except that the dust covering Ben's face had been black. In those days people would often visit the cottage, calling in whenever they needed their chimney swept.

'Just wondering if you could swing by later,' they would say.

Or, 'I reckon the Council'll be onto me soon.'

And nearly always, 'Yeah, I wouldn't say no to a cup of tea.'

Those were the things she missed. The regular things. The everyday. Everyone in Kurow appreciated Ben; without him, she was just a strange sculptor. Ben had brought the community inside. His parents had left Kurow after his death, the Dam where he'd collapsed, a chilling reminder. Her eyes dampened. She ran her hand over Luke's hair and the dust that fell in a melancholic path to the floor allowed her to feel at home, making her mark.

He took a tattered book from under his pillow. She didn't recognise it but when he opened it, she noticed that the words on the withered pages were large and interspersed with pictures. She curled her body and rested her head onto his stomach as he read it out loud, distracted from his words by the gurgle of his insides. Her guilt for enjoying the warmth of him made her feel nauseous.

The lantern flickered slightly as he read. His voice stayed flat and he paused only to breathe. Then, without warning, the narrative stopped. Delia opened her eyes and realised the lantern had died.

'That's all there is,' he said.

'Don't you have a torch?' she asked. It didn't seem fair to stop now. The bit about the nomad in the story reminded her of their previous conversation and she realised that he'd modelled himself on the character.

'I do, but . . .' his voice trailed off and he showed her where the story had ceased at the end of the page.

She ran her fingertips over Luke's stomach, and raised herself up to look at him. His outline was blurred. 'So why did you read it to me if the last pages are missing?' she asked.

His voice became further muted. 'I wanted to ask you what you think happens to him.'

'Don't you already know?' she said. 'Surely you've read it before.'

'I have,' he said. 'Again and again, but the pages are missing.'

'They blew away?'

'Something like that.'

'Does that change the ending?'

'It could.'

She considered this for a moment, raised herself up further and lowered the full weight of her body onto his. 'I think,' she said hopefully, 'that he returns home.'

She noticed him sink with her weight. He shivered and she knew he wasn't cold.

'Surely a nomad character wouldn't return home?' he said.

'That's not what they do – they continue to travel forever.'

Delia's face felt heavy. It occurred to her that maybe, just maybe, she didn't want Luke to leave the lakeside. 'Why did you ask me if that's what you've already decided?'

'I wanted to know if I was right.'

She was glad of the darkness. It hid the glint of the tear that she wiped away. 'Only you can decide that,' she managed, 'but one thing you might consider is that the pages are missing for a reason.'

'And what reason is that?'

She chose her words carefully, selecting each from pockets in the dark. 'So that you can invent your own ending.' It was what she was doing.

'That's what I thought too,' he said. 'I just wanted to see if you thought the same.'

He closed the book's cover and placed it once more under the pillow. The stones beneath the tent dug into her back.

'I heard of someone once,' she said.

'Yea.'

'He reminds me of the person in the story and of you.'

Dust returned to cling to them, and in the shadows, Luke appeared as an old man might, an old man who'd pedalled until he was too old to pedal.

'He had amnesia and he didn't know who he was.'

'Aha.'

'So he started moving from one place to the next as if trying to figure it out.'

'Was he living out of a tent?' He laughed. 'I think sometimes artists' imaginations get away from them.'

She didn't know which clung to him more tightly – her fingertips or the dust.

The following morning the tent filled with a sticky heat. Delia awoke dehydrated, her sleeping bag stuck to slimy skin. She reached for a water bottle and gorged its contents, and as the final trickle edged its way down her throat, realised she was alone. Her finger traced the outline of where he had lain. She remembered the delight of her weight on his, and that in that moment it hadn't mattered that they were stuck in one place.

The humidity surrounding her was stifling. She unzipped a corner of the tent and looked out at the beginnings of the day. The stale air released itself and a refreshing cool flowed in through the gap. She saw Luke sliding his way in and out of the lake, his muscles adjusting to the variations of each dive. He dipped in and out, spending more time below the surface than above.

She unzipped the tent further and wove her way across the stones. Her toes met the water and curled. The sun kissed her bare figure. Taking a few steps into the water as it submerged her thighs, she dived holding her breath, kicking, the chill gathering around her and banishing the humid heat that clung to her. In one fluid motion she met him under the water and clasped onto his shoulder. They rose and took a breath, gasped but didn't speak, and then he smiled and pulled her under again. Their two naked figures twisted and danced beneath pale water, unseen by anyone except fish.

Afterwards, Delia sat on a towel and dried her body below a broad sky. She wore a wide-brimmed sunhat that shaded both her face and her thoughts. Her skin stopped glistening as it dried. She recollected an unsettling phrase from the night before: 'a nomad wouldn't return home . . .'

Ah well, she thought, if that's the case then, neither might I.

AUTUMN

4

Delia emerged from the thin pall of the khaki tent door. Her hair clumped together in thick straggly twists and was drawn over her face like a gathered curtain. She traced the outline of the hills with her finger. It shook with hunger. She wasn't sure how many days and nights had gone by since she'd moved to the lake. Three perhaps, or five, maybe longer . . . She and Luke had repositioned the tent twice, each time closer to the Dam.

Luke had set off to forage for mushrooms and said he would be back soon. He'd erected a fishing rod in a holder, its line cast out to depths below, searching for prey. She looked at it and noted that it was motionless. Her stomach churned. She longed for food. Beyond that, there were other things she missed too. The simple everyday comforts that, from her cottage, she could so easily have. A shower. Her chisel and mallet. A piece of stone. Anything and everything beyond this.

She walked into the water fully clothed, humming to herself. The chill surrounded her, removing the grime she'd accumulated – a rank viscous layer of sweat. She had become feral. Her sundress splayed out in the water around, light and led by the currents. She lay on her back challenging the sun to burn her face. With her ears filled with water the sound of her hum was muffled and distant. She sank below the surface, holding her breath, and when her lungs started to ache she pushed back upwards greeting the air.

She turned her head towards the shore. The fishing line twitched against the backdrop of glittering water. Her eyes might have tricked her. It jerked again. She surged her way through the water, feeling a sharp sting underneath her foot. Whatever tugged on the end of the line continued to fight and swagger its way around the lake and try to hide beneath darkened crevices. She reached the line and began to pull it. A dark muscle writhed around her in fluid whips. She grunted and heaved. The leaden body looked sickly against the pale water and it squirmed in panic, its gills longing for reprieve as it struggled to stay submerged. The shadowy snake of slime bit at her, cutting her arm while she yanked the line, wielding it with a guttural yell out of the water.

The eel squirmed around so violently she worried it might slither back into the water. She held tight to the line, pulling the eel further onto the shore, and attempted to grab its tail but it snuck beyond her grasp. Still holding the line, she leveraged the eel's weight by pressing her back against the nearest tree trunk. Little by little, she wrapped the line around it, then in a quick motion, let go of the line, took a large rock and heaved it onto the eel's body. The rock and the tautness of the line held it pinned. She pushed the rock along its body to its head and straddled it, holding tight to the eel between her knees as she raised the rock and brought it back down. She hit at it again and again. At first the hulking figure kept twitching but slowly its mangled body stilled and blood began to seep out to stain the stones. She stooped over its dead body. A trail of blood led to the water's edge. Her arms were scratched, bruised and torn and the fishing twine had cut across her palms. Her sundress dripped in a circle around her.

Her heart rate refused to slow and she panted. The Four Square wasn't so far away. She could have gone there, bought a supply of bread and jam, visited a butcher and bought some meat like a regular woman. She thought of how fish bought from a market looked so peaceful, their expressions in death the same as a day before in life. The eel's eyes were marred beyond recognition.

Delia looked around for Luke but couldn't see him. She found a flattened rock and heaved the eel onto it. She curled its body to fit, laid some leaves over its unsightly face to offer dignity and positioned some stones around it into a frame. She began to sob between her breaths, purging herself, gouging at her shame.

. . .

Luke gathered the mushrooms into a pile by his feet. He took a knife from its sheath and squatted, not quite ready to return to the campsite. Taking a stone he ran the blade's flat side over the edge and began to sharpen it, counting strokes on either side. When satisfied, he took another stone, brushed it with his fingertips to check that it was less coarse than the first and repeated the action. He used the newly sharpened edge to trim his nails, which he collected in a pile and scattered into the lake. The half-moons floated along a little way then sank. A cut filled with blood and a droplet fell to the stones.

He could see Delia but she was far away and blurred, wading into the water. He turned his head away to where the lakeside was empty, as it had been before. Delia was always nearby now. It had become rare for him to look out at the landscape without seeing her figure moving within it or in his periphery. During times when she was further away, she reminded him of the pylons, gaunt and worn down. It seemed that one day the lake might wash her away.

The trees dotted around Kurow had turned terracotta and ginger. Streets were laden with fallen leaves, fluttering striations of autumnal colour. The air was mild and malleable, broken by interchangeable breaths of warmth and chill.

Jane stood at the door of the cottage. The wisteria wrapping around it curled together, closing its entrance. The weatherboard gleamed white beneath. She knocked heartily but heard no response, imagined an imperceptible shuffle of bare feet on boards and after a few moments, knocked again. She retreated from the entrance, concerned. It was unlike Delia to stand her up.

The following day she returned at the same time and discovered the cottage empty once more. A foreboding quiver ran through her. She walked slowly around the perimeter of the house and saw that the studio window was agape. A familiar scent lingered at its mouth. She looked about, wary, and found herself completely alone. The other houses in the street appeared empty and ghostlike. Not a single lawnmower rumbled.

Jane took a few tentative steps towards the weatherboard shell of the house and raised her body up onto a jutting tree root. Her heart reverberated in her chest as she visualised Delia spread-eagled in the studio surrounded by lethal tools. Raising her head above the lip of the window she breathed a sigh of relief. Delia wasn't there. She could be elsewhere inside the cottage and for reasons unknown, not responding. Not seeing her, she slithered her way painfully through the mouth of the window frame and lowered herself to the floor. She didn't feel guilt at her intrusion; she felt as if she'd returned home. The room was littered with statues of herself. She mused at the idea of visiting old friends. In the centre of the room the beginnings of a new statue had started to take shape. A tinge of jealousy ran through her. She walked briskly to stand in front of it, her footprints separating a path through the dust. The statue was moulded into a meditative stance, relaxed and without an ounce of vanity. She thought of her own figure posing in front of Delia, holding a variety of positions, all of which were staged. This statue didn't seem staged. She ran a finger lightly over its cheek, caressing it and felt for a moment that she had lost her breath. She wondered whether the sculptor had done the same. The statue looked to her to be very familiar as if it was someone she knew – somebody who had taken her place.

Leaving the studio, she walked around the shadowed interior of the house. Her chest felt heavy. She found Delia's bedroom in disarray, clothes scattered in green and brown mixed piles. Lying uninvited on the bed she stared at the ceiling. Her heart pounded. She smelt the light scent of Delia's hair on her pillowslip.

You were always just a body, a mystery, she heard a voice whisper in her ear. *What is your name?*

Jane.

Plain Jane.

She turned her head sideways, listening. Through the open door of the bedroom she saw another door ajar and realised she had never seen inside this particular room. Curiosity stabbed at her. She raised herself off Delia's bed, leaving an impression on the duvet, and slipped across the hallway.

The room was laden with books and statues, and these statues, she realised, held a close likeness to the one in the studio. They appeared blurry though, as if unfinished. Her eyes, too, glazed over, the dust and the murkiness of the room making her feel claustrophobic. She exited the room, her body heavy, and made her way swiftly through the house and out of the front door, careful to hear it latch shut. The sound took her by surprise; the street remained eerily quiet. Not a single parent sizzled eggs for breakfast. No dogs barked.

Her feet tapped as she walked along the pavement, around a corner and past the primary school. It was a school day but she couldn't hear the giggles of any of the children. The jungle gym was just the same and the asphalt where all the children sat each day to eat their lunch.

It was here that Jane used to watch Luke holding his lunch-box filled with sandwiches and cherries. He sat alone. Pips of cherries fell in a semi-circle around his feet. His hands were sticky and stained. The cherries looked delicious, but she was too embarrassed to ask for one. On her first day at the school, she too sat alone, her cheeks flushed as other children played. Her mother had packed her a juice box and she sipped on the straw, the sweetness playing on her taste buds, leaving an aftertaste.

A group of girls giggled and swung each other around. They saw her perched on the bench. 'C'mon,' one had called. 'Come and play.'

She got up and stood awkwardly amongst them. The shyness soon subsided and she became embedded within their group, sitting each day in circles to chatter, running around on the field and swinging on the jungle gym, spinning their sundresses into jellyfish.

Each day she'd noticed that the boy continued to sit alone, staring into space or wandering around kicking his heels, not playing with the other boys. The pile of cherry pips on the ground increased. Why, she wondered, did the caretaker never sweep them up? She had never seen such a lonely sight, the boy sitting solitary against the backdrop of others playing, his knobbly knees clenched together. He never joined the games of cricket or rugby. He never wrestled. Sometimes he sat with a book.

The girls ran around on the field until they exhausted themselves, and lay on the grass looking up at the clouds, their Roman sandals thrown into muddled confusion around them. They'd return home with a different pair each day.

One day, Jane's friend Amanda started to pluck at the grass and daisies, creating a collage on her splayed out skirt.

'Who is the boy always eating cherries?' Jane asked.

'I don't know.' Amanda concentrated on plucking a daisy and holding it in the air.

'That's Luke,' another piped in. 'He's a loner.'

'Yeah.'

'Other boys tease him because he's weird.' They'd giggled.

The girls moved on to talk about other things. Important matters. And then the bell had rung and that was that.

. . .

Paprika-coloured leaves skittered along the street. Needing respite, Delia returned to her cottage alone. An image of the bloodied eel had taken residence in her mind lurking in dark cavities. The ghoul-like creature must have waited for nightfall before reawakening and slithering through the tent and into her gaping mouth. She needed a shower to wash the effect of the lake from her, if only for a few moments.

She noticed a familiar car parked in the drive and felt intruded on, conscious of her tatty appearance and matted hair.

Her mother emerged from behind the rear of the cottage,

walking swiftly. 'Ah, Delia,' she exclaimed, 'I was just popping by to check.' Her mouth fell open.

'I was away at the lake for a swim,' Delia responded airily. She fumbled in her backpack for her key, hastily sorting through an assortment of clothes in need of washing whilst attempting to hide the bag's contents.

'Seems you've been gone a few days,' her mother remarked. Her own attire was well kept and crisp.

Delia took hold of the key, triumphant, and unlocked the door. 'I'd really like a shower,' she said. 'Do you think you could come again later?' She walked through the door, keeping hold of it, ready to close.

Ignoring that, her mother stepped through into the hallway. 'I'll wait,' she said and strode ahead, her manner decisive.

Delia heard the kettle being filled and a click as it was switched on. She sighed. Helen would have to wait.

In the bathroom she opened the window wide. Her travel-weary sundress fell to the floor in a stained heap. Standing in front of the mirror, she saw her cheekbones were more prominent and her face glowed olive. She took a pair of scissors from a cupboard and cut at the unsightly clumps in her hair.

The shower took a little while to heat. She stood underneath it but found it difficult to relax. An ache grew as the eel within her settled; she had hoped it might become attracted to the scent of the water and slither out of her. The thought made her feel nauseous. She leant against the wall, letting the water wash over her back, calming her, then turned the shower off. In the kitchen her mother continued to wait, likely swallowing black tea between exhalations of impatience.

Delia entered the kitchen, wearing a new dress and with her

hair tied back, unusually sensible looking. She pulled up a chair at the kitchen table and sat, adopting a calm persona and a straight posture, her head tilted sideways as if listening attentively.

Her mother's finger tapped on her mug. 'Delia,' she began, 'you know I'm here for a reason, don't you?'

Delia ignored this. 'The exhibition will be ready soon,' she said.

'I'm here because –'

'Would you like to see the progress?' She stood up quickly, her calm façade diminishing.

'I'd like you to see a professional.'

'A professional?'

'Someone who can help you.'

Delia squinted, then forced her expression to regain neutrality.

'A psychiatrist or psychologist.'

'No, no,' Delia said in a silky tone, 'that won't be necessary.'

'Just to talk about Ben,' her mother said. 'It couldn't hurt, now, could it?' She looked at her. 'There are many stages of grief.'

There was a pause as Delia pretended to consider this, one eyebrow tilted. 'I'm fine. You don't need to worry.'

She smiled, like the model, posing.

Her mother stared at her as if in disbelief and turned to leave.

Night spread across Kurow, a long note refusing to farewell a sorrowful tune. The village resisted. The shadowed half darkened first, then the second half followed suit. Delia's cottage turned from white to grey. The light within lessened imperceptibly, casting her studio into a glum atmosphere. Shadows began to creep up the walls and sneak into the crevices between the statues, their curves becoming prominent.

Relieved to be alone, she walked between the statues of the model, one stretched with her arms to the sky, her nails now off-white and ghostly, her stomach flat and bare and her limbs elegant. Delia had been too absorbed in the task to allow her respite. Her fingertip ran over the statue's arm.

She took her chisel and began to chip away at it, severing the femininity, allowing it to become abstract. The dust glided over her fingertips, settling in her cuticles. Chunks fell to the floor. She carved at the body of the statue, attempting to make it masculine. This proved difficult. Too much was already chipped away. She would need to make it smaller to make it masculine and this didn't equate.

Time slid away and the studio darkened further. Shadows merged into each other. The sparse population of Kurow retreated to their beds. Delia did not. She remained awake, chipping stone, the chisel and mallet guiding her thoughts. Her fingers were calloused from the repetitive action. The dust became dizzying and she wandered out of the studio to make herself a cup of tea.

She returned to the studio and sat on the floor, looking at the statue she'd altered. As she drank, the caffeine loosened the weariness from her eyelids. She switched on a light and the studio began to glow. The tea tasted powdery like her surrounds. She drank it quickly, her body hungry but not craving food.

Delia placed the enamel cup on the floor and moved it gently, carving a circle in the dust. She stood to resume her work. The chest had become masculine and smooth. The hand that once curled into the air – elegant nails reaching towards a sun – had become a male hand.

She began to change the face, the chisel's blade clinking against the stone. Hours stretched, the night reaching its long tentacles into the room. The face resembled a sinister combination of the model and Ben, making her heart pound and her stomach nauseous. Even as objects in her memory the pair were together still. She persisted through her fear, her fingers rubbed raw by the sandpaper, erasing all remnants of the model until finally only Ben's face remained.

The final surface she sanded lovingly then stood back from her work. Took in the entirety of it. His eyes stared back at her, reassuring her. She dared him to awaken.

The physicality still didn't seem right though – Ben would not pose like this. He and the model had been together, never really apart, even after death. She too was still together with Ben, but unlike the model, she had a way to bring him back. Shaking her head she stepped away. The pose was that of the model – seductive, and one she could not erase.

5

The sky above Aviemore was posing too – honey coloured instead of blue. Luke arrived back at the campsite with a hessian bag half full of mushrooms and was surprised to find Delia absent. He found the eel curled in a circle, covered in a variety of mustard-tinged leaves, though beneath the leaves deep-red blood had wept onto the stones. A note on a torn piece of paper held down by a frame of sticks and stones read:

Here's your dinner. I'll be gone a little while.

He ran his fingers over the skin of the eel. It was tough and slippery indicating a recent capture. He decided to cook it for his lunch, his stomach chewing at his insides. After retrieving a knife from his backpack he slit the skin just below the gills, circling its body. The skin parted easily. He grasped it and pulled it back, loosening it with the knife occasionally to ease its passage. Gutting the eel, he used the knife to cut along the membrane of the backbone and fillet it. The remnants he discarded, tossing them into the lake. He then cooked the eel surrounded by mushrooms, the smell of its flesh searing and the earthy vegetables wafting across the campsite.

He allowed the cooked eel to cool for a couple of minutes and then raised the first morsel to his lips. It was a shame Delia wasn't there to share the meal with him. Their days at the lake could not continue and it was time for him to move on. It wasn't fair of him to steal her from normality. The food served a functional purpose; he was no longer able to enjoy it.

He began to pack, stuffing his pillow case with clothes. He changed his mind, pulled them out and folded them, then picked up the painted stone that lay in the now empty space on the canvas. 'I'll keep it with me wherever I go,' he had said, but this was soon to become a lie. He passed his fingertips over the fine brushstrokes, appreciating the effort Delia had spent. His chest was heavy. He might not return to Aviemore and had to leave this reminder of what had once been.

He emerged from the tent, lowered his body and cast the stone into the lake. It skipped three times before settling in the layered depths, triggering an ache of regret. He completed his packing, the eel in his stomach churning and making him feel ill.

His bike lay awaiting him in the grass. The claret colour it had once been was chipped and replaced with smatterings of rust. He hauled it from its slumber and started to pedal. He didn't dare to look back.

After he'd been cycling for a while, he passed the orchard where he'd spent his childhood, his pulse quickened, and he didn't look sideways then either.

∫∫∫

The orchard fringing Kurow gleamed, its trees laden with black-red cherries. Luke looked out from inside his bedroom window at the grass dappled in jigsaw shapes of early morning sun. Cherries bobbed, bursting with sweetness.

His father called.

He stood, made his way to the kitchen and sat at the table.

His feet dangled underneath it, then grasped onto the legs of the chair, taut. Three chairs surrounded the table, one empty. His father placed an egg on his plate and two pieces of toast; he sat staunch, his feet cemented to the floor, his legs spread. They ate in silence, staring at blank walls. Their hands were stained with the ink of cherry skins; their bodies weary from an arduous season. The sun sapped their energy each day and the work was monotonous. Luke's arms still ached from yesterday as he ate his egg.

He heard the click of utensils on porcelain and a squelching chewing sound. He listened to the whoosh of coffee swirling in and around his father's teeth, discolouring them. A sliver of sunshine glinted through the curtain and began to bake the earth around their home, sucking at the meagre moisture the night had provided and searching for more. A clock ticked, marking the repeat of routine. His father stood and clomped to the sink, thrusting his plate into it. He swirled the remnants of his coffee and swallowed, then left the room.

Luke sat for a few moments, enjoying the solitude. He looked at the now second empty seat and his legs released their tension. His plate was covered in a sheen of yolk and smatterings of crumbs. He cut a trail across it with his fork, creating a road with an unpleasant gnawing sound. His fork swivelled and he drew the orchard, row upon row of trees, their roots searching for water, and branches reaching upwards. He gathered the crumbs into the shape of a figure walking along the road away from the orchard, then stood up to rinse his plate in the sink. The crumbs crept off the plate and made a pathway out of sight.

Today, like every other day during the holiday, he filled buckets, layering the bodies of cherries on top of each other.

In his dreams cherries fell as rain and surrounded his bed, while each day branches cradled and trapped him. Light that seeped through the trees whispered rumours of other settings beyond the orchard, which may or may not exist. He heard these whispers but pretended not to.

He piled the cherries, careful not to bruise them. They emitted the red of winter rosehip, deep and seductive. They teased him by being alluring, but exhausted him by begging to be picked. Occasionally one would pop, its sticky juice creating a veneer over his fingertips. The pigment in the skin of each cherry soaked into his pores. Often he would eat a handful or two and then need to find a spot under the trees to dig a hole and relieve his bursting bowels.

Many hours passed before his father checked on him. He glanced in the buckets but just said, 'Dinner.'

Luke slid from the tree, his darkened hands blending into the bark. They ate, again quietly. The awkward tinkle of utensils rang a familiar tune.

∫∫∫

The lake's reflections were skewed. Luke laid his bike in the grass. Weeping willows swayed their tips in the water, left and right. The soles of his feet connected with the stones. They were jagged underfoot but familiar and comforting. The water caressed his toes. He looked down to see his own image, also swaying and blurred, making him appear younger. It was encapsulated there, murky and confused, pinned beneath the stones. It reminded him of his youth, filling buckets with cherries. His father had spent his whole life at the orchard, it'd been passed down from his father and his father's father. It hadn't been fair of his father to expect Luke to live the same life and he had never been able to shake the feeling of resentment. Alfred had called him selfish – when really, all he'd wanted was freedom. The sort of freedom he had now. He thought of a passage he'd read many times in the nomad book.

When I die I'll be a bird . . .

Stepping back from the edge of the lake, he pulled his bike from the grass and did as he always did – continued to pedal.

Delia.

He thought of her instead.

The bike wheels carved a line through the stones and he watched as his reflection was mirrored onto the lake, moving along its surface. Away. As always, away.

6

At some point Delia must have slept. Bright light awoke her. It was afternoon, her body clock altered. She was pleased to be alone and wished to properly reacquaint herself with her cottage, feeling guilty for having abandoned it.

The dust in the kitchen had accumulated since her sojourn at the lake. She took a broom and swept at it, carving a path. It gathered in clouds around her feet coating them with familiarity. She wiggled her toes, causing wafts of dust to resettle, the previous night's severing of the model's statue an insignificant memory.

She traipsed from room to room. Her mother's departure had been abrupt, and the chair she had sat on, tapping at her black tea cup, was now empty.

Her statues greeted her as she passed them by. The studio window was wide open as she had left it, and beneath it was the statue of Luke, poised in a meditative pose. She raised her hand to his cheek and brushed it with her fingertips, imagining the statue standing up and filling with colour, his meditation over now that she'd entered the studio.

Luke hadn't been able to sit still, not for long enough, but he would, later, certainly. She took a piece of fine-grained sandpaper and delicately rubbed the statue's arm. The sandpaper pressed in her hand was reassuring, a tool by which she could shape her memories.

Luke would have discovered the eel by now and considered her whereabouts. She couldn't stay apart from him for long. She took a step back from the statue. Although unfinished, unlike the statues of Ben, this one appeared more lifelike. It had been modelled on someone tangible. Someone who maybe, just maybe, she was beginning to care for – or could more than care for if she allowed herself. Her heart warmed a little and she smiled. She brushed the dust against her own cheek, leaving a smudge.

Smiling, she headed for her bedroom. It didn't matter which way her life flowed and for once this didn't perturb her. She had been given a taste of freedom. A tattered notebook lay open on her bookshelf. She found the model's phone number, lifted the phone receiver, paused for a moment and dialled. Her sentences came out in a flurry as she made her apologies. The model responded, seeming nonchalant.

'Jane, I was wondering if you're free at all today?' The name didn't roll easily off Delia's tongue.

'I can come now, if you like.'

'Really?'

'I don't have any clients this afternoon.'

The model had some other clients, old folks – she cleaned for them, showered them. It was irritating because there were a few times she wasn't available.

Their conversation petered out and Delia replaced the receiver. The model would arrive in an hour. Before she resumed her work, Delia needed to hide her night's project with a sheet. She hoped routine would normalise her life again.

She thought of the eel curled on the rock and the disgust she once had felt dissipated, replaced with pride. She'd battled the eel and won. Challenged nature and fought to survive.

The model arrived shortly afterwards. Unlike usual sessions, she didn't remove her clothes. Her dress stayed loose around her. And then she did an odd thing. She positioned her body into a meditative position, exactly as Luke had been seated, mirroring the statue in front of her. She settled into it, raised her lids and looked at Delia, defiant.

'Is this how you remember it?' she asked and she closed her eyes.

. . .

With her eyes closed Jane listened to the tap of the chisel breaking the stone. Often, when being sculpted, her thoughts didn't stay in the room, instead seeping back to the orchard where she as a young girl had hidden behind a cherry tree, her fingers pressed against the texture of the bark. She'd seen Luke high aloft a branch facing away from her, a bucket perched in his lap. Jane watched him with curiosity. If she were closer she'd be able to hear the patter of cherries falling steadily into the bucket as he worked.

Pull, pick, drop.

Pull, pick, drop.

He'd appeared weary and maudlin.

Around lunchtime a deep voice lured him back to the house through the trees. She tucked herself closer to the trunk, blending into it. He walked past her, his head lowered, his bare feet patting through the grass. If he'd found her he might think her a tree nymph and wish to become friends. He hadn't. As always, he was oblivious to her. Her stomach rumbled; she too was ready for lunch. He must have been one step too far away to hear.

She wound her way through the maze to the base of the tree

where he'd been perched, high on a branch above where she was now. She thought to climb the tree herself, and look out over the orchard, see if she could see him sitting at the kitchen table through the window. He really seemed to like eggs. She knew this because once or twice, when her nerves had dared her, she'd snuck close to his house and looked inside. A stern looking father lived there, but the mother must have been ill or something because she was never up and about. Every time the boy and his father had been eating eggs, just sitting there and not talking to each other.

He'd left the bucket at the base of the tree and she could see it was only half full. The cherries inside were perfect with no bruises or dents. She took one in her mouth, where his fingertips had been, and chewed it. The flesh burst readily and lined her tongue with sweetness. She rolled the pip around on her tongue. The bucket being half full didn't seem right. She took to the task herself, hanging the bucket around her neck with its leather strap, clambering up the tree, selecting and pulling cherries and filling the bucket. Cherries gleamed a deep black-red. Luke would be back soon. She shimmied down the tree and left the bucket upright on the grass where it had been, then hid again. The leaves formed a familiar hideaway for her voyeurism. She was still hungry and the single cherry had not been enough. It was tempting to sneak back to the bucket and take a handful but she thought it best to stay put.

Eventually he'd returned, his father clomping along beside him. She breathed lightly as she peered through the leaves.

'Got much done?' the father asked.

'A bit.' Luke kept his head low. His voice was so quiet she could barely hear it.

The father peered over the bucket, his shoulders hiding her

view of it. 'Blimey,' he said. 'Not bad.'

As Luke struggled to hide his surprise she withheld a giggle.

Jane had retreated through the trees and wandered along the road. Her Roman sandals had worn thin over the holidays but no one at home noticed. When she returned to school and played on the field with her friends their sandals were discarded and splayed out. The other girls noticed which ones were hers, the tatty pair. They didn't swap with her any longer. They went about selecting pairs which looked nice and that their mothers would approve of.

No one at home noticed anything much really, not important things like that, and today, like other days before, not even the fact that plain Jane was gone . . .

The tapping had stopped and Jane opened her eyes but she struggled to see Delia through the haze. It was then that Delia began to talk, faltering, her words floating through the dust like lonely pebbles struggling to float.

• • •

Luke's progress was slow. His bike carving a ponderous path along the side of the Otematata highway, weighed heavily with pannier bags. The road followed the southern bank of Lake Aviemore, clinging to it. The weeping willows turning brilliant shades of burnt orange interwoven with caramel reflected on the still surface of the water they hung over. The cool temperature of autumn helped to cool him as he rode. He passed over the Aviemore Dam, waving it a farewell. His eyes were blurred. Salt gathered around his lashes.

The road emerged onto the upper Waitaki floodplain. To his right the river's braids stretched and curled into the distance, soil carved as if by chisels. Having made an unexpected decision, he rode in the direction of Kurow, not towards Omarama as he had planned. Delia would inevitably find his campsite empty, he knew this. He wanted to see her one last time – but only see her, not talk to her. If he hadn't been such a bloody fool, he wouldn't have become so attached. He lay his bike in the grass near her cottage and, as he approached, found the door ajar. He stood at the entrance and listened, surprised to hear a familiar woman's voice.

'I think that maybe you need to let him go.' The voice was measured, followed by a pause. 'If you keep making statues of him, you'll never be able to.'

'What do you mean?'

'Your mother told me about Ben, and that he'd passed away.'

'It's no secret. You must have known him too, didn't you?'

'No. I . . .'

He swiftly shuffled into the hallway, careful not to allow his footsteps to be heard. A second door he found open. He entered and found a library of sorts filled with statues.

'This statue is how I remember him,' Delia said.

'Like a photograph.'

'I suppose.'

He lowered himself, breathing quietly, into a squat on the floor.

'Did you sculpt it from memory?'

His heart hammered, it was him that had posed to be sculpted, not Ben. Was she talking about the sculpture of him or another? She seemed to be describing him as if he were already gone, lost and ghost-like, a memory to be clung to. It jarred him. To this point he had been staring at the carpet, not taking in any details. Now looking around the room he took a few seconds to adjust to what he saw. The statues around him were mirror images of him. Their expressions were different but their features were the same. The room and the statues began to melt blurring his vision. He gasped quietly, unheard, realising he'd missed some of the conversation.

'The others, though. The other statues. He wasn't here for those, was he?'

He heard an intake of breath and strained his head forward.

'Excuse me?'

'It's just . . . I'm sorry, Delia, I saw the other statues too.'

'When did you?'

'I thought . . . well, when I came the other day and you weren't here. I was worried about you, so I came in.'

He heard Delia's voice rise in pitch. 'You mean you came into my house? Looked around?'

There was no response.

'The door was locked.'

'I came in through the studio window.' A pause again. 'Listen, your mother had asked me to keep an eye on you. I just thought that you might have needed my help, been in trouble.'

The statues around him shook their heads in worry, mimicking his shock.

'I didn't mean to pry, I just –'

'That room is private.'

He heard a slight scuffle, a quick pacing of feet.

'The statues there, they weren't so lifelike. Almost unfinished.'

'So?'

'You didn't have a model for those, did you?'

'You're wrong.'

He listened to their emotions undulate.

'I'm sorry.'

'Are you seeing things Delia?'

He clasped his eyes shut.

'Because if you are, there are people who can help you.'

'Those statues are old. I sculpted him long ago.'

The rest of their conversation became a blur and the woman, whose voice he knew to be Jane's, made her excuses to leave. He tucked his body behind the crook of the door. She walked swiftly. He kept his breathing quiet, tried to still himself like the statues, become frozen. He'd met Jane at the lake too, a couple of months before he'd left Kurow, and it grated on him that the two women knew each other. Kurow was too small.

Delia entered the room, curled herself into the chair and began to weep, her body shaking in great spasms. He remained tucked in the corner, unable to help her and confused.

She cried the sort of grief that only emerges when a person is alone. He realised he didn't really know her at all.

It took many hours before Luke was able to retreat, unseen, from Delia's cottage. He waited for her weeping to cease and clenched his eyes shut as she left the room. It was as if by ensuring he couldn't see, she might not see him either. He waited, hearing her busying herself in the bathroom. The shuffle of her feet as she returned to her studio. A half-hearted tapping at stone.

His bike awaited him and he cast himself onto it, pushing off. It was time to go in a direction away from her. Tips of trailing wisteria waved him farewell.

The hills surrounding Kurow were oppressing and close. He sought a road to stretch in front of him, one with a vanishing horizon, to forget all that he had heard, and remember Delia only as an innocent stranger at a lake.

Large trucks passing him along the highway vibrated the

road beneath his bicycle wheels like miniature earthquakes reverberating with his unhappiness. He ignored his aching calves and followed a line of power lines. A cluster of dam houses erected with stone blended into the landscape. He passed paddocks full of river stone, cairns of piled rocks, collective pasts of locals and tourists.

A car on the opposite side of the road slowed and a familiar face looked at him through a barrier of glass. It took him a moment to register. He shook his head in apprehension and surprise. The car gurgled onto the gravel at the side of the road. The driver's door opened and his father, Alfred, stepped out.

'You didn't make it far from the orchard then.' The voice reverberated across the road, deep but not loud. Alfred walked towards him, not pausing to see if traffic came from either direction. 'I thought you'd have made it to the North Island by now, or left the country.'

Seeing him, after his experience at Delia's cottage, was too much of an onslaught. He gripped tight to his handlebars. 'I wanted to come back for the summer,' he replied, his words broken.

His father paused. 'The orchard was here this summer too,' he said. 'I couldn't pick it all, not by myself.'

Luke stayed astride his bike. The weight of the pannier bags pressed against his muscles. 'I couldn't do it anymore.' He held himself steady, staring at him, direct. 'I can't do it anymore.'

'What do you mean, you can't? You can't means you won't.'

Luke considered this and shook his head. His father reminded him of the entrapment of the orchard. Cherries falling and gathering on the soil around him until they piled on top of each other, reaching upwards to his throat, attempting to drown him.

'It means I can't.' His voice pitched, defying his show of

confidence. 'The same routine day after day. No escape.'

'So you just run away?'

'Yes, I suppose so,' he said. 'For as long as I have to. Is it any different to how you continue to work? Blocking out your loss by picking cherries?'

'Of course it's bloody different.'

'Continue to work and forget how to live.'

His father had aged over the duration of his absence. His skin was toughened like leather, having suffered one summer too many, and the loneliness had wizened him. Luke banished a pang of guilt.

'I want you to come home,' his father said.

It was almost a plea. One that did not exonerate him. So Luke did what he always did – he started to pedal. 'I can't.'

It was too much, all of it.

He cycled with his heart pounding, and the adrenalin made him feel like drums and maracas were pounding a tune inside his chest. Seeing his father again reminded him of his days as a teenager. Back then too he had heard the pounding of drums and maracas, the miniature instruments beating an insistent tune in an offbeat to the time of his bedroom clock. He could still see and feel every moment of that day as if it were yesterday, standing in front of the mirror in his bedroom, so that he could see himself from head to foot. He'd replayed it so many times.

∫∫∫

His knobbly knees poked out from a pair of oversized grey shorts and his uniform hung loosely on him, making his gangly figure look gaunt. His stained hands were fidgeting with a hole in his jersey; his fingers trembling a little, sending a wave of electricity coursing through him. The horizon fell away into nothingness in the distance.

He bent and picked up his schoolbag from the floor. It too was faded and second-hand. Its brown dusty colour blended with the wooden floors. Pulling it onto his back, it weighed little, containing only cherries, sandwiches, an exercise book and a blunt pencil. He walked a few steps towards the mirror, practising a confident stride and, after a few attempts, opened the door and left the room. His stride remained fake-strong but his hands still shook and the instruments kept jangling. He could hear his father clattering away in the kitchen and poked his head through the door. The kitchen was dim, mimicking a glum routine. Two eggs gently tinkled as they boiled. The sharp aroma of black coffee filled the room.

He lowered his backpack and sat in his chair. His father didn't turn to face him, just wiped the bench vigorously as if trying to remove the top layer. The boiling water enveloping the eggs threatened to spill over the pot. He yanked at the pot handle and poured cold water over them and after a few moments picked up the scalding eggs and plonked each onto a plate. He drew a knife from the drawer and leant over the sink with his shoulders stooped, his face shadowed, emotionless. He cracked and cut through the eggs, crushed shell dangling precariously into the yolks.

Luke ate. The taste didn't reach his tongue. He waded through the fragments of broken shell. The instruments continued to pound an unsettling tune and the noise grated at him. His father stared at the wall. He chewed at the soft flesh.

'There'll be just as much work. Make sure you come straight home. I can't do it all myself.' The words gyrated between chewing sounds.

Standing and hoisting his bag onto his back Luke looked at his father who swallowed a final defeated gulp, and realised the man no longer looked terrifying. He was broken. The realisation had lessened his ominous appearance. His hands, wiry and hardworking, were becoming wrinkled. Coated below his eyes was a layer of pallid shadow. The skin sagged a little where gravity pulled at his sockets.

Luke made a path towards the doorway and didn't dare turn back.

He trailed away from the orchard into the bright crisp morning, following a path lined with off-white stones. They rubbed against each other. His weight bore on them causing delicate crunching sounds. The trees waved him a farewell. He made the same path away from the orchard as he had once drawn with the yolk on his plate; the same boy moulded by crumbs, who had decided to leave and not return. He walked slowly, meandering along the path, relishing the release. The instruments in his chest quietened and ceased to remind him of his fear. It was nice to imagine that he wouldn't return, when really, as usual, the school bus would pick him up and drop him back off at the end of the day.

He waited beside the road until the waiting became tedious and then kicked some stones to pass the time. The grass swayed sideways to the road and then up at the sky, back and forth. He could hear the bus approaching long before he could see it, a deep ponderous sound and the lowering of gears. He imagined the raucous conversation of teenagers inside and then did an unexpected thing.

Ran.

He ran away from the bus and back into the confines of the orchard. The trees gossiped and giggled at his actions, brushing their leaves. He lowered his body to the ground, listened to the inhalations of his breath and the rumble of the bus as it approached. It slowed for a moment or two, the sound humming, and then resumed its escalated rumble back to motion as it trundled away. The grass tickled his belly.

He emerged from his hideout and trudged in the opposite direction to the bus. The empty sky stretched wide over his head. Jaundiced grasses swayed in empty fields, smelling of cooked earth. As he walked, the damp cool of the morning warmed and dried. Dust covered his school shoes. He sat in the grass contentedly and removed them. The grass and dirt felt exquisite between his toes.

A truck came into view, its belly full of sheep heading to their slaughter. Luke stood straight, his naked feet hidden by shrubbery. He pretended to look for an approaching bus, one that he knew had already passed. The truck driver tipped his hat at him and passed by. The truck's rumble had disturbed the stone quiet for only a few moments.

He tucked his shoes into his backpack and continued to walk. As his steps lengthened and the heat of the morning increased, he removed his school shirt too and walked along in a singlet, his shoulders catching the glare of the sun. He walked in the direction of Aviemore away from the fear of the orchard, and did not care for consequences.

He whiled away the day, following the road. The school routine he was supposed to be taking part in ticked on. Students wrote into exercise books and made cheeky quips at their teachers. He was glad to be on his own path although his shoulders burned and he struggled with the glare.

When he reached Aviemore he ate the food in his backpack,

then stared around absently as if waiting for the next event. He listened to the lake breathe, in and out. Cherry pips surrounded him and a few floated at the edge of the water. The remnants of their flesh leaked juice into it, sweetening it. The edge of the lake kissed his feet.

It was necessary to make plans. He wondered where he might sleep when night fell and what he might eat now that his backpack was empty. The area was exposed apart from the cover of a few trees, however, his most pressing challenge was how to conceal that he was a schoolboy. He needed to appear unkempt, as a traveller might. The school shorts he still wore were an alarming giveaway. He would have to keep himself concealed. Luckily, so far only the truck driver had seen him.

Perhaps the shorts, if dirtied slightly, might appear like regular shorts. He gathered some dust and rubbed it in, leaving a bruise on them. The disguise didn't seem sufficient. He took some grass and plucked it, then rubbed again at the same area. The tendrils of grass left a secondary stain. His backpack too seemed a giveaway to his identity but was also a necessary item if he were to travel the country. He held it in front of him. The school emblem appeared to glow like a highlighter on a page. He searched on the ground for something sharp, a stone or a stick. Nothing immediately caught his eye. The stones were smoothed by the lake, and the sticks, dried weak by the sun, snapped under any pressure. He scavenged the ground in an ever-increasing arc, eventually sighing a long exhale of exasperation. He then returned to his backpack and pulled the emblem closer to himself. His fingers yanked at it, attempting to wangle between it and the canvas. The stitches didn't budge – they must have been stuck tight with glue.

Frustrated, he realised he would have to discard the bag. It would be no use to him if it gave him away. A heavy rock fragmented by chips appealed to him. He hauled it, along with his backpack, into the water and weighed the bag down, drowning it along with his former life. The emblem was beneath the rock, disguised to anyone who might happen to gaze on the water.

He panted. The exertion of carrying the rock and the heat of the day were starting to wear on him. His skin tingled and his head ached as he lowered his near-naked frame and supped at the lake. He splashed himself in its cooling refreshment. His head continued to moan at him.

The trees surrounding the immediate area were straight and astute, offering no shade. He began to feel as if he was shrivelling, weakening, eaten ravenously by the sun. A few hundred metres away a pair of weeping willows beckoned to him. They shaded the fish that swam in the cool water but offered little reprieve at the lake's edge. The weeping willows would have to suffice. They reached out beneath the surface towards him.

He started to wade, his thin legs dredging through the water. The trees seemed to stretch further away from him and he felt light-headed. They swayed and he swayed with them, taking part in an involuntary dance. Then, just as he felt he might reach them, his mind swirled and he fell. The branches caught him and cradled him, adopting him. They held his mouth just above the surface of the water. Their leaves wept around him, moving delicately with the currents.

The lake returned to its equilibrium, going about its business as if he didn't exist.

ʃʃʃ

The mountains in the distance appeared two-dimensional against the sky as if cut by scissors. His body whirred as his bike lilted over a cattle-stop, dodging potholes leading a trail along the side of the airfield. Rosehips, snarly and warped, glistened like jewels. Omarama greeted him with a new beginning. Lake Aviemore now a distant memory.

He located a new spot for his tent just outside the airfield behind a row of poplar trees, and an oak laden with acorns and fairy caps. Evening had fallen and the glider pilots had locked their elegant crafts away into a hangar for the night. He was glad of the privacy and noted a few rabbits scuttling around. Hunger gnawed at him.

He pulled his gun bag from within a pannier. The pieces of the gun inside were dismantled into two. He screwed the stock back onto the receiver and pieced it together expertly, as a soldier might, the routine habitual. The metal barrel was dull and cold. He felt the weight of it in his hands, loaded a round, locked it up, and cocked it. He spied a rabbit in the grass and started to stalk it, aiming at its head. He followed its movements for a few seconds, eyeing it through the sight. It sniffed at the ground and he shot it behind its ear. The sound of the bullet ejaculated through the barrel and into its victim, ping-ponging across the hills. The rabbit bled little and died instantly, its stomach slumping onto the ground and its nose pointed at the earth. Its eyes were locked.

Luke cocked the block open and removed the casing in the chamber. He rested the rifle against his tent, glad not to have wasted the bullet. Its gaping mouth was warm with triumph.

He took a knife and rubbed its blade on the grass, picked up the rabbit's body with its rear end pointed to the ground, and squeezed its bladder so its piss fell in a trail. He wrapped his hands around its upper body, tightening his fingers, forcing its organs low. He pressed further until the belly became bulbous, appearing as if it might burst. The entrails fell through its anus.

With his knife he began to skin the rabbit, slicing the blade through its fur, trickles of blood falling between his fingers and staining the earth. He broke the bones and cut in a circle, chopping off the paws and head, then ran a line down its belly. The pelt came off in one piece leaving the carcass naked. He laid it onto fallen leaves and covered it to waylay the buzzing of flies. He buried the entrails and pelt beneath the roasted earth, the dust clinging to his sticky hands.

The sun had begun to set. He dug a pit hurriedly on a bare patch of earth, creating a fire with dried grass, moss and twigs. It lit eagerly and he added layers of thin branches. His earlier worries seeped away; he shed the skin of a peculiar day and basked in self-sufficiency. Guilt fell around his feet.

When the rabbit was cooked he laid it again on the leaves and allowed it to cool. His stomach would be full soon, it would have no reason to complain and burble at him. He cut the flesh, tearing strips, and raised the first mouthful to his lips. The consistency was chewy, as was often the case with the wild animals he caught, creatures free to roam and utilise their muscles. Poplar trees swayed, providing a backdrop between his tent and the hills. Shadows merged into each other as night settled.

He slept a deep sleep that night. The day's journey and events had left his body in need of repair. He dreamt of Delia twirling around him in a sundress with a wide-brimmed sunhat forming shadows over her face. He danced with her but then became tired and as still as stone, his figure locked into a meditative pose. He couldn't escape the feeling of being trapped in stone as she circled him, tapping at his skin with a chisel, and tried to tell her it hurt and she should stop, but couldn't.

He rose early. The grass of the airfield sought a drink in the dust but an azure sky offered no reassurance of rain. The enormity of it rendered him insignificant in its space. Eager pilots had arrived at the airfield and begun opening their hangars. He listened to them, jealous at their freedom to take flight, explore the hills, and dance with each other through changeable currents of air. He unzipped his tent, yearning for a lake to dip his body, but instead sat cross-legged and watched them through the poplar trees, an admiring observer with life passing him by.

Delia would have come with him here. She would possibly have come with him anywhere. She was nuts though, he knew that, yet in an odd way that didn't bother him. Some of the most interesting people he'd met during his journey had been completely bonkers. They were the ones who were happy enough to sit and chat with him, a homeless guy who couldn't stay put.

He distracted himself by beginning to tidy his new campsite, arranging his meagre belongings. A conundrum waylaid him. Where the heck had he placed his gun? He was certain it had been propped against the tent.

Had it fallen down?

He searched alongside the tent, beneath it, around it, between the poplar trees, at the site of the buried entrails and the spit.

Had he imagined eating the rabbit?

Dreamt it?

He opened each pannier bag wide to no avail. Luke shook his head in frantic confusion. The gun was gone.

· · ·

For the last few days Jane had taken a daily drive by the lake, but she hadn't been able to see Luke's khaki tent. At first she didn't worry. He might have positioned it behind a sprawling weeping willow out of sight, but now, she knew he'd gone. Again.

Like the time she'd sat on the school bus, waiting in vain for Luke to get on. Then, like now, she had wanted to find him.

She returned to Kurow by way of the orchard, missing the elusive boy who had once been hidden there.

Usually Luke waited for the bus at the beginning of a pathway leading into the orchard. She was picked up two stops earlier, and so, each week day, she would already be sitting in the bus before he was collected. A couple of years had passed since she'd started at this school and he hadn't missed a beat. He never greeted the bus driver as he stepped in, and he sat alone at the front; he never looked up and certainly not at her. It seemed he didn't notice the world go by or want to get to know the other children.

Over the last couple of years, the boys had stopped bullying him. He had become as familiar to them as the desks and chairs, an object that moved about sometimes but seldom spoke. He was considered a little peculiar but harmless. Jane didn't stop being curious about him though. She followed his movements and tried to contemplate what he was thinking about. She didn't attempt to speak to him; he seemed too distant, as if by speaking to him she might make him run. He was a fragile enigma, one that she would like to protect but didn't know how.

On the last day of the school year, the bus had dropped him off at the entrance to the orchard and she'd watched his dwindling figure turn and walk down the path through the trees. His head was lowered and she imagined that his face was solemn. She never saw him in the town and he didn't go to the lake to swim. He'd walked down that path, away from the bus and the orchard had locked him inside. When the new school year dawned she would be attending intermediate and so would he.

After the holiday, she'd sat near the front of the bus, running her fingers over the cracks in the leather of her seat. Her uniform was new and crisp. She felt anxious but not because of the change of school. The bus slowed, the gears passing through their downward routine, and drew to an idle outside his usual waiting place. The space was empty. She'd cast her stare around the surrounding trees, as if he might emerge from a different location, marking his new intermediate maturity with a confident flourish. Even the bus driver seemed a little confused and lingered at the spot for a few moments longer than necessary.

The bus then resumed its regular rumble and as it drove off, for a moment, she thought she'd seen the glow of their new school emblem sticking out from beneath one of the cherry trees, attached to a bag and near the path. But the bus had driven off quickly and she was unable to take a second look.

This time she knew that he couldn't have gone far. He was hiding again, or running. Jane pulled her car over to the side of the road, pebbles and stones splaying sideways. She'd parked close to where she knew he had last been, so close that she could see the patch of grass dehydrated by the shape of his khaki tent, a bleached shape left behind by Luke who did as he always did, packed up and moved on. Away from her. A single hawk passed a shadow over the cadence of the water. It might be that the hawk was leading in Luke's direction, or forewarning her of something she couldn't quite grasp yet. That's silly though, she thought, hawks are everywhere in this area of the country, part of the scenery. They didn't hold any hidden meaning. Her hopes were as usual resting on emptiness.

. . .

Delia closed her front door and latched it shut. The air was laden with chill. She walked away from her cottage. Its white gleam had turned dim. She narrowed her lids. Moisture settled on her fingertips and drizzle coated the outside of her jersey in tiny droplets. She wrapped her arms closely around her, thinking of Ben strolling beside her. His hair had grown and his apparition looked different to how she remembered him, perhaps more like Luke. He changed a little each time, becoming less real, as if he was slowly fading away. His hand brushed hers and she reached out gently into the open air beside her.

Passing the bingo club, she raised her head above the window frame. Chortles permeated through the glass; chatter, the loud ding of a bell. Nestled amongst a cluster of heads striated grey and white were busy hands. The odd face turned, recognised her, and she waved.

At the petrol station the scent of gas was dizzying. A pair of teenage boys pulled up to the side of the tarmac in a low-slung car, its engine's drone contrasting with the stillness of the empty road fading into the distance. One stepped out to fill the tank, his pants slung low. The town was livelier than usual.

She wandered the streets and familiar pavements. She didn't want to shift away from Kurow, but if she was ever going to move on from her memories she'd have to. Ben was here in her recollections. In her cottage. Walking the streets. Visiting his grandmother at the bingo club. In every puff of smoke that emerged from a chimney. Trust her to have fallen for the town chimney sweeper. He hadn't had grand aspirations and she had loved that about him. He was humble, a person the town had relied on. A part of the community that she now felt so separated from. He was human here, real, and now she didn't want that anymore because he was gone.

Days quickly blended into each other and Delia hadn't yet returned to the lake. She missed the sheer freedom that accompanied the solitude of it, and quickly forgot how feral she had become during her few days there. The appeal of accompanying Luke, the recluse, beckoned her again.

She showered, the warmth of the water passing over her, brightening her spirits, cleansing her. Then, refreshed, she drove in the direction of Aviemore, to a site she had developed an affinity for. And to see Luke, who gave her the hope that she could start again.

The journey passed quickly. She located where she had fought the eel, discovering the campsite empty. This didn't perturb her; it wasn't likely that Luke would have remained in the same spot. She turned in a full circle searching for him but couldn't see him. The weeping willows glowed amber, the autumnal surrounds taking on a fresh personality, startling and bright.

Finding him wouldn't be too hard. Her feet trailed along the edges of the lake. The water brushed at her ankles, sending chills through her. She wandered for an hour but still couldn't see him. The outline of his tent had become invisible, his claret bicycle hidden beyond her view. She nestled herself atop the stones. Perhaps Luke had relocated his camping site in the opposite direction and she would need to retrace her steps. He could have hidden his tent behind a tree and in a moment of reverie she'd missed it. It occurred to her that since she'd been gone he had been alone as she was now, at peace with his isolation. He hadn't sought her or needed to. The lake loomed and a melancholic ache started to form in her gut. Could it be that he was no longer here, that he'd left without a care for the fact that she would return? The seed of doubt began to grow. It stung. She forced it away and, despite her lethargy, stood up and continued to walk.

Her steps were more frantic now and she no longer airily trailed her toes through the water. Sweat clung to her and made her shiver. Stones seemed to position themselves in her way, causing her to stumble.

She staggered away from the stones that hindered her steps, lowered herself into a bed of rusty leaves and closed her eyes. Light played beneath her eyelids, an ochre glow reminding her of summer. Aviemore melted. Leaves gathered around her feet. She rocked back and forth, the stones in front of her jingling. The air around her becoming cooler and she wrapped her arms around herself. Twigs chafed her cheek and caught in her hair splayed outwards in a tangle. Her body crumpled, sinking further into the ground. She snuggled into her jersey, the wool clandestine against her, so furtive her shivering skin ceased to acknowledge its existence. Her thoughts slipped further into wary disorientation. She would stay the night at Aviemore and find him in the morning. The lake wouldn't mind. Its edge was her home now.

. . .

The streets of Dunedin were busy although the awkward transition between autumn and winter had begun to darken the place. Unlike Aviemore, fewer golden trees warmed people's spirits; shadows were strewn and footfalls collided with moist streets. The outline of Dunedin Hospital was the tint of ash.

Helen perched in the waiting room. The walls surrounding her were sterile and cold. She was ushered into an adjourning room where a doctor sat, surrounded by office paraphernalia. His coat looked ironed crisp and he gleamed, in the way doctors do. He removed the coat and placed it over his chair, revealing a brown cardigan with patches on the elbows. His nose sported a pair of spectacles. He came across as more human now, less a cookie-cutter product of society. He was young, she noted, but had a wise glint to his eye.

'We're sorry it has taken us this long to contact you,' he said, 'but it took a little while to figure out her next of kin.' He leant forward in his chair. 'I'm sure you've been very worried.'

She wound the tassels of her scarf around her fingers. 'I don't know what to think,' she said, 'what to do. I've been worried about her for a while.'

'Understandably so. I'll need to ask you some questions about her behaviour.'

'Of course.'

He smiled a reassuring smile. 'As you know, Delia was found with bloodied hands and feet, as if she had been walking barefoot for some time and perhaps stumbling. Having spent the night in the open she is also mildly hypothermic and we're treating her for that.'

She breathed in heavily. The weight of the event rested on her shoulders and she wondered what she could have done to prevent it.

'We'll treat her physically first.' He paused. 'But then,' he paused again, seeming to measure the information he fed her, 'I think it'll be necessary to consider giving her some time in the psychiatric ward.'

His words filled the corners of the room and glued themselves there.

She nodded. His suggestion did not come entirely as a surprise.

His green eyes glowed against the white of the room, calming her. He seemed to genuinely care.

Helen straightened herself. She resumed her usual persona, however much the act was false, placing her hands together in a prim manner. 'The problem is, doctor,' she began, 'I know my daughter and she is very stubborn. She won't stay anywhere she doesn't want to be and what's more worrying is that she won't admit to needing help.'

She let the information sink in. In this moment it was she who needed help.

He removed his spectacles and placed them on the table. 'These things are never easy,' he said, 'especially if the patient refuses assistance, but . . . the mental health team are trained to deal with circumstances like this, with individuals who . . .' he held her gaze, 'don't know they're ill.'

Helen remained poised, listening, holding her dignity between her hands. 'If she isn't aware she is ill, though . . .'

'Compulsory treatment is available for those who may be at risk of harming themselves.'

'I see.'

She thought of Delia trapped behind white walls, and then as a young girl building statues out of clay in the garden, covering herself in mud.

'She will undergo a psychiatric assessment so we can ascertain her level of mental health.'

'I see,' she repeated.

The doctor's eyes held her steady, preventing her from falling off the chair. 'It may be that she has simply had a breakdown of sorts.'

Simply.

The doctor loosened his gaze and looked out through the window. Dunedin residents bustled by, running their errands, leading their lives. The distant chime of the clock tower marked the beginning of his lunch break. Another morning slid by and another patient had fallen under his care.

At the end of the day Helen left the hospital, its gaping mouth awaiting her return, and made her way towards her motel room. Compared to Kurow the streets were alive with sound. A group of students sauntered along, swinging beer cans by their sides and hollering across the road. The clock tower in the Octagon chimed again, marking the passing of another hour, momentarily interrupting the chatter of a group of hipsters leaning over their coffees. They sported beards and hats of various assortments.

The smell and noise of traffic jarred her senses as cars grumbled and drivers behind iced glass waited for the lights to change. Red. Green. Then a blur of movement and rust. A scooter wove sideways ridden by a woman, lace tails trailing behind her.

The outline of Helen's motel was charmless. It was painted a faded vomit yellow that must have once looked cheery. The doors opened automatically and, as she walked in, the burr of the city fell away and became a background mumble. The proprietor nodded at her and looked down, importantly ruffling papers. The woman's skin was pale and Helen noted that the papers were blank.

Once inside her room she latched the door shut, switched off the light, removed her outer layers and crawled underneath the coverlet. The clothes formed a reminiscent cairn-like pile at the base of the bed. Her scarf on top of the pile reminded her of a time she had sat in the sand at Karitane Beach with Delia and how she had thought then that if only they could get away, all would be well. Beneath the doorway, the hallway lights buzzed a little in an unnatural way and formed an angle of light across the carpet. The place felt aseptic like the hospital.

She exhaled and closed her eyes, the doctor's words tapping across the insides of her lids. She thought of his elbow patches, his spectacles and his words jumbling, confusion between image and sound. She breathed in, attempting to clear the jumble, missing the scent of Karitane's salt air. At least there she could have gone to the beach, if only for a few hours to get away, carrying her daughter or walking with her hand in hand, their progress slow.

Many nights had been lonely there, when Delia's father had passed out on the couch, or hadn't returned for hours from the Waikouaiti pub, leaving her surrounded by trees and shadows and salt air. Even though they'd run away – first to North East Valley – nothing had improved.

The hills of Dunedin's North East Valley had shadowed the street as Helen walked. Delia would be home soon and she had to hurry. The bus would drop her daughter off near their rental house and Helen had been excited since this was Delia's first day in high school, her uniform creased for the first time. Well actually the uniform was second-hand, but Helen liked to imagine she had bought it for her daughter new. She welled with pride.

Helen wasn't, of course, allowed to meet Delia off the bus – that would be far too embarrassing. She would have to wait inside and pretend not to mill around near the window frame. The house had been damp and she'd wished she could provide more for her daughter. Delia didn't seem to mind though. She occupied herself by sculpting clay during the weekends, the kitchen table often strewn with newspaper. She wasn't so good at cleaning up after herself though. Helen unlatched the door, switched on the kettle, sat at the kitchen bench and waited.

As was often the case, she was suddenly struck with fear. What if she was left sitting here, waiting, and then had to call the police? What if her daughter didn't return home?

The night she'd taken Delia from Karitane she'd been so afraid. She'd worried he'd follow her or set the police on her. But, he hadn't. The first day passed and no search party had chased them. A second day went by and then a third. He must have known it was right for her to take their daughter, although little did he know she hadn't managed to take her very far.

Tap.

Tap.

Tap.

Delia's footsteps. The door opened.

'Oh, you're home,' Helen said. 'That was quick.'

Her daughter grimaced. 'Yeah, yeah.'

'Was it okay? Did you meet some nice people?' Helen leant forward. The kettle had boiled to a crescendo. Her hands shook beneath the table.

'Everyone goes to high school, Mum. It's no big deal.' Delia dropped her bag and slouched off.

Alone again, Helen stilled her hands and gazed out of the window. The sky was pale and charmless. She'd contemplated her next steps, how in a few years she might be able to take her daughter further afield. To somewhere warmer and remote.

Somewhere safe and empty.

Helen couldn't sleep. She opened her eyes again to stare up at the motel ceiling. Shadows flitted across its surface. A gap in the curtain flashed light occasionally as the odd car hummed by. Insomnia was something both she and her daughter shared. She sat up, pulled back the covers and reached beside the bed for her hand bag; she took her cell phone from it and saw that she had two missed calls and a message. *Helen*, the message read, *you've missed two shifts now. Is everything alright?* She'd forgotten completely to say that she'd be out of town, and why. It was strange to think that other people's lives and routines were still going on, as hers should be. She began to type a reply to the message but then stopped. It wasn't right for her to be tied down to any job, she'd worry about that when she got back to Kurow, when she knew her daughter was healthy again. Also, if she moved from job to job frequently then no one would be able to find out where she was. Maybe instead she could work at one of the orchards and get cash in hand. Her benefit wasn't near enough. Her stomach gnawed at her and she realised that part of the reason she couldn't sleep, besides her worry for Delia, was because during the day at the hospital, she hadn't thought to eat. And couldn't really afford to. This is madness, she thought, to stay strong for Delia she had to stay strong for herself – even if it meant getting into debt. She dressed again, ready to go outside and pass by the drunkards of the city to find a twenty four hour dairy. Relieved, such a small task gave her purpose.

· · ·

From Alfred's angle the road pointing towards Omarama in the direction his son had gone stretched into a triangle, fading from sight into a point. The sky above it was pale and lilting. Alfred hadn't driven off straight away. He'd leant against his vehicle, contemplating following Luke, watching the claret bicycle become blurred into a dot as it reached the point and vanished. He was gone again, so soon.

Alfred sat in his car for a little while, passing cars reminding him of the direction he must go. He decided to wait and follow in the direction of Omarama; it was the likely choice for a camping site. He lingered for what felt like an hour, his fingers drumming on his knee. It wouldn't be possible for Luke to make it too far. His bike was laden with camping gear.

He sparked the engine, his decision to follow Luke solidified with sound, and drove slowly, surrounded by a hazel and apricot landscape. The horizon looked as if it was moving away from him as he drove, like the boy on the bike, out of reach.

When he arrived at the outskirts of the Omarama airfield, evening had started to descend. The mountains were adorned with jagged shadows. He walked beside a line of poplar trees. They rustled, spurring him on, covering his path with dappled silhouettes. The trees led him in the direction a camper might go, looking for the perfect location to retire for the evening.

A shot reverberated against the hills. He might have found Luke but could not yet see him. He followed the course of the sound, weaving his way between the line of trees, careful to keep quiet and concealed.

Some way off he saw a person – a hunter perhaps or a camper. He lowered himself into the grass and camouflaged behind a tree. The figure held aloft a rabbit and was squeezing at its innards. Although far away, he knew the camper must be Luke. He crept closer and watched as the rabbit was expertly skinned. It might have been pride that he felt, pride or shock. He wasn't sure which. He recalled Luke younger than this – innocent, lazy, hiding behind the trees in the orchard avoiding work, or school. A car passed by and for a moment he thought that he saw the constable's face looking out at him. It wasn't though, the face was that of a stranger. He closed his eyes. An image of the orchard rose in his mind. It shivered as a breath of air chiselled through its lines of trees. They chattered to each other, the breeze passing a message amongst them, a car grumbling its way into the drive. Alfred had lowered himself from his perch to the ground, surprised to see a police car.

'G'day, Dennis,' he'd called, pondering the unexpected visit of the local constable.

The constable appeared too crisp to suit the orchard setting. He'd turned his head in Alfred's direction and nodded, then opened the back door to his vehicle. Alfred had shaken his head in disbelief at what he'd seen. Luke slowly getting out of the car, his shirt gone and his shorts dirtied. His hands clasped a bucket and his head was stooped over it. He'd appeared wet and bedraggled, feral.

'He has a bad case of sunstroke, I'm afraid,' the constable had said.

'He's got what?'

'He was found by a couple of campers at the lake, passed out.'

'What? Why? He was supposed to be at bloody school.'

'Well . . .'

Luke, hearing the murmurings describing his capture, seemed to wither. He'd retched into the bucket, sinking into a kneeling position, then retched some more, producing little more than a few droplets of bile.

'Didn't go to school,' Alfred said, as his son continued to heave.

'He's only just started bloody high school – what are they going to think?' Embarrassed, he launched into a tirade of colourful language, watching as Luke edged towards the house, his steps hesitant and his upper body bent.

When the police car departed, Alfred made his way into the house, his heavy boots drumming at the floorboards. He'd found Luke lying on his bed, dampening the sheets. His body was curled weakly into a protective circle. The glint from the sun through a gap between the curtains was hitting his cheek, and his eyes were wincing. His head drooped, unable to stay lucid. Alfred had sunk himself into a squatting position and propped Luke's head up with a rough, stained hand. The boy shrivelled at the touch.

'It isn't bedtime,' Alfred said. 'You'd better get up and clean that bucket. The day's work isn't done.'

He strode towards the window. The curtains squeaked open and light stabbed into the room. His shadow as he returned made the boy's skin appear grey. It masked a clammy sheen. Alfred passed a rough hand over his son's head and Luke appeared to relax, if only for a moment, and closed his eyes.

'Not sure what you were thinking, running off like that.' He stood up, sighing and clomped away.

The car that passed along the roadside had long since faded into the distance. Alfred hung his head.

• • •

The air above Omarama airfield was piercing. Luke watched the gliders circling the skies. Their broad wings passed shadows over his tent as they headed into the abyss, seeking lift, spiralling through waves of air. He envied them.

Curiosity led him through the gap between the poplar trees,

his bare feet leading a path to the airfield. He sauntered around its edges, finding a glider unattended. Its long wing to his right nestled in the grass and it glinted at various angles. He circled around the glider, pausing to gaze through its canopy.

'She's a beauty, ain't she?'

He turned and saw a chubby man in Stubbies approach him, grinning. 'Sure is,' Luke agreed.

The man pulled a cigarette from a packet and held it as one does when in the habit of it, limp and sticky between his two fingers. He lit it and a puff of smoke rose in an evaporating cloud above his head. He looked down his nose at Luke, assessing him. 'Been travelling for a while then, eh?

'You could say that.'

The man sucked on his cigarette. 'You look like you could do with a feed.'

Luke thought of the rabbit he'd killed the previous night. How chewy the meat had been and how regular foods, like sandwiches, had become a luxury. His body was wiry and thin, strong yet always craving his next meal. He nodded.

The man continued to grin. 'The missus,' he said, 'she made me some lunch, but it was all bloody health food so I ate a pie.'

'Oh.'

'I was going to throw it away but –'

'No, I'd make use of it,' Luke cut in.

The man sucked for a final time on his cigarette and then squashed it into the grass. 'Thought you might, mate.' He pulled a lunchbox from a backpack and passed it to him.

Luke settled himself onto the ground beside the glider and opened the box. He was amused to find the various foods neatly arranged in segments, like a child's lunchbox. He ate some raisins, the sweet fruits heavenly as they connected with his taste buds.

The man in the Stubbies squatted beside him. 'I reckon you could also do with a shower, mate, but I don't have one of those around 'ere.'

Luke ceased chewing on his raisins for a moment. He was particularly grimy – there was no water here to take a daily bath in. The airfield was only a temporary home. 'I'll be leaving tomorrow,' he said. 'Heading to the lake.'

'To Aviemore?'

'No, possibly Benmore, or somewhere I can take a dip. The Ahuriri River, perhaps.'

'You don't have a plan?'

'That's the joy of it.'

'How long have you been on the road then?'

'A while.'

The man chuckled. He stood and circled his glider, making a series of checks, tinkering. Luke ate his unexpected breakfast, glad to have made a new acquaintance. He finished the final sandwich, savouring it, storing the energy for a time when food would not be so abundant. The quiet tinkering of his unhealthy new friend soothed him. He glanced around to see if the man was watching and sneakily picked up the cigarette butt, wrapped it in cling film, and placed it in the lunchbox, not wanting to leave litter.

'So, have you been gliding for a while?' he asked, mirroring the pilot's question.

'You could say that,' the man wheezed, pulling at cables beneath the canopy.

'Are you going up today?'

The man pulled his head out from within the body of the

glider, sweat sheening across his forehead. 'Why, mate, would you like to come?'

'I sure would.'

'Righto.' He paused, considering. 'Well, we're going to need a bloody jacket on you so I don't keel over, but alright.'

Luke grinned.

7

Delia's eyelids flickered open and then shut, open and then shut again. She slowly roused herself and became acquainted with her new surroundings. She hadn't awakened at the lake as she'd expected to. The water did not lap at her toes and the morning sunshine did not greet her.

She propped herself up, disorientated, feeling the stinging tug of a drip in her arm. The white walls around her blushed too brightly and her head ached. She felt trapped, held tight by sheets that clung to her skin. A figure sat in the chair in the corner of the room, dozing or perhaps sleeping; it was hard to tell. It wasn't her mother visiting her as she would have expected. It was the model looking different to when she did whilst being sculpted, less like an object now she was wearing clothes, more human. Delia studied her face, long lashes teetering on waxy cheeks.

Shuffling noises in rooms nearby stirred the model. She turned her head sideways and opened her eyes. Their pupils met, locked.

'Oh, Delia,' she said, moving to the bedside, 'I'm so sorry. Your mother was here and I just thought I'd give her a break, watch over you for a while.'

'Watch over me?'

'She was so very tired and . . . and I thought I could help.' She now stood directly by the bedside. 'Tell her if there was any news.'

'News.' Delia turned her head away, nestling into the pillow, her eyes blurry. 'About Luke?'

'About you.'

'Oh.'

'You were found passed out at the lake.'

Delia closed her eyes, vaguely remembering a pair of hands hoisting her up.

'That isn't too unusual – I live there,' she said, the comment a deliberate provocation.

The model hid her shock well, leant forward. 'I'm so sorry, Delia,' she said, 'about what I did.'

'You.' Delia sat up, her demeanour suddenly changed. 'It was your fault.' She strained against her drip, her hands shaking.

'I wanted to check that you were okay.'

'He will never be the same because of you.'

'What are you talking about? I'm sorry I came into your house. I . . .'

Delia wrenched free from her drip, clasping her hands around the model's neck, yelling as they both toppled to the floor. She visualised the eel whipping and whirling around her, and the model's body blended into her memory of it, waxen and thick.

Orderlies quickly entered the room, pulling the two women apart. The cuts on Delia's bloodied hands reopened as she strained to break away from them. The orderlies, dressed in pale blue, a tangle of arms, full of strength, held her to the bed. Others pulled the model away, her face contorted in anguish.

Then Delia's arm stung, the room became hazy, and the orderlies didn't need to hold her down any longer because she fell, or sank. Her body refused to move, though she strained for it to do so. Murmuring, 'it was you, I saw . . .' she slipped out of consciousness.

• • •

At Omarama, while waiting for their flight, Luke's new friend had smoked five cigarettes. They passed from his lips, one after the other. Luke soon gave up trying to surreptitiously pick them up. The airfield must have been littered with them, hidden by dry grass.

'The thing about gliding, mate,' the man said, reclining in the sun, 'is that you do a lot of waiting around. You might spend half an hour in the sky and twelve hours on the ground.'

Luke didn't mind; he too reclined on the hardened earth and watched the gliders soar above him. Their wings took turns to glint depending on the angle of the sun as they circled.

'Is there any reason you're on the run, mate?'

'Not as such.'

'Not a convict on the loose, are ya?'

'Not as far as I know.'

'Girl trouble?'

'Something like that.'

A puff of smoke rose into the sky to join with the clouds. The man looked at him quizzically. 'You must be struggling for money,' he said. 'Even escaped convicts need to buy the odd pint or two.'

'Maybe I won the Lotto.' Luke smiled.

He breathed in the scent of good fortune, reclining.

A car slowly pulled a winch cable to their glider. Their turn had come. The car was rusty and weather-beaten, idling along with a straining hum. Luke felt a rush of nerves. He'd become accustomed to his sedate lifestyle at Aviemore, very different to this.

His new acquaintance puffed and panted. He pulled up the glider's front seat and hoisted what looked like a lump of lead into it. Luke was about to be thrust into the air with a man who might well have a heart attack.

'Hop in and strap this over you, mate, and be sure to clamp it in the middle. I don't imagine you weigh much, so I plonked in some ballast.'

Luke's wiry frame reached easily into the body of the glider, his feet touching the pedals. He didn't take up much of the space, unlike the man behind him, who squeezed in with a grunt.

'It's about evening out the weight in the front and back,' the man continued.

The canopy stayed open, waiting.

Luke listened as the man ran through a series of checks and closed his eyes. The pilot seemed to have adopted a serious side to his personality. After a while, he heard a click as the pilot pulled the back canopy shut.

'You gotta shut the lid.'

Opening his eyes again, he did so. He pulled at the canopy, clicking it shut. The scenery seemed to magnify as he looked out from within the bubble of glass.

'Brakes: open, closed, locked.' There was a pause as the glider rattled a little, the brakes popping open on the wings and then closed. 'Check.' He heard the pilot shuffle in his seat. 'Now mate, I must explain what happens in the event of a cable break . . .'

Luke swallowed. He heard the words of the pilot that followed but didn't listen, and when the man's voice petered out, he took a deep breath.

'All clear above and behind. Take up slack.'

He felt a tug.

'All out.'

He opened his eyes. The glider careered a short distance along the length of the airfield, picking up speed. Luke felt the rumble of the earth beneath him and then nothing. Omarama fell away. The glider's unfamiliar angle pulled at his cheeks and stomach. The earth had vanished and all he could see was emptiness. There wasn't time to admire it; their journey upwards was staggeringly swift.

They reached the release point and the pilot pulled the bung. Somewhere far below them the cable fell and was wound in. Luke felt the controls move between his legs. The pilot behind him was turning the glider sharply. The wing tip carved a line over the edge of the horizon. He made a steady path towards the hills, pausing from time to time to circle in columns of lift, riding the waves in the air.

Luke tried to find his tent, a khaki dot somewhere far beneath them, but the take-off had disorientated him. Through the canopy, the world appeared magnified. An air vent to his right hissed as it breathed delicately on him. Otherwise, there was silence.

They flew along the ridges of hills, littered by shadows, upwards and away. The pilot was curiously silent. Luke took a deep breath.

The glider was straightening out of the bank and after a few moments it looped upside down and his stomach curled towards his throat, his weight pressing on his shoulders against his seatbelt. Omarama stretched below him, wide and stunning. The horizon shifted and expanded. For a moment he caught a glimpse of the curve of the earth. A broad and stretching arch. The burnt amber trees formed a backdrop to the opal they played in.

A few days passed without Luke seeing the pilot again. The leaves, tinged brown at their edges, started falling in dainty succession, like intermittent rain showers. They settled, forming a dried and crisp mustard carpet that shattered into shards as Luke walked, forming a path beneath his feet. His toes were cold, on the verge of numb. They had lost their summer resilience and each step sent shooting pains through his bones. He rubbed his hands together in a feeble attempt to keep them warm.

The sky was stark above him as he left his tent and belongings perched on the edge of the Ahuriri River to await his return. He stood on the roadside, his thumb in the air as cars passed him by, waiting for an hour or so, and then a station wagon slowed. The driver wound the window down and Luke's eyes widened.

He smiled but felt his cheeks blush. He and Jane had had a summer fling before he'd left. It hadn't meant much to him – he'd liked her but wanted to get as far the heck out of Kurow as he could.

She smiled back. Maybe she wasn't mad at him. A lot of time had passed.

'Hello, stranger,' she said.

She told him that she was heading to Oamaru and asked if he'd like to join her. Luke was glad of the company; he had spent many a solitary night since his glider flight. He closed the passenger door, and as she drove off he watched his tent fade away.

'You've been gone awhile,' she said. 'I didn't think you'd come back.' The car swerved a little.

'Neither did I.'

'Been waiting long? For a lift?'

'Not much.'

Her skin was clear and matt, as if it had been sculpted and

sanded to perfection. She was a lot more confident than before, so maybe not everyone in Kurow stayed the same. He'd changed a lot too, he thought. He'd been just a silly boy then.

'Where are you heading?' she asked.

'Well, anywhere that I can buy a pair of boots.'

'Oh,' she smiled. 'Oamaru should have those.'

At one point she pulled over, saying she needed to stretch. He stayed in the passenger seat, warming his feet. Jane faced away from him to the side of the road, her breath curling into the air. She stretched in what looked like a pose, her outline curvaceous and seductive, more than he'd remembered. He felt intrusive and lowered his head, staring instead at the floor of the car, allowing himself to calm.

She returned to the car, eased herself into it and sparked the ignition.

'I guess you're not visiting Oamaru for shoes then,' he said.

'No,' she replied, 'I have a client there.'

She let the information hang in the air but seemed reluctant to add to it.

. . .

Delia roused to find the hospital room empty. Her hands and feet were locked to the bed somehow. She writhed a little then settled, staring up at the ceiling, letting a moment of peace sweep over her.

The walls glowed in an unearthly way reminiscent of the inside of Luke's tent, as if the room were expanding and magnified. A blur lingered over her pupils, passing like a river and subsiding as she woke properly. The stale air wrapped around her, lingering in her lungs. She heard footsteps pass by her room, the squeaking of shoes on vinyl, coughing, and the insistent ringing of a telephone.

The world outside chattered away and forgot her.

An image of the eel whipped through her memory, the model intertwining with the creature and becoming one mass of grey muscle. She cast her eyes to where the model had been and the empty chair reassured her. She attempted to curl into a ball and failed; her hands and feet were locked tight, irritated by the leather. She closed her eyes and let the haze settle.

After some time, a nurse came and untied the bonds. Delia's hands and feet moved around like an octopus, splaying out. They stung. The nurse left; her hands had been gentle and her voice soothing.

Boredom soon set in. She met it and welcomed it. She carved a statue in the air, one known to her. She chipped at it with her chisel, the texture of the handle blocked by bandages. Layers of dust and stone fell in disarray around her bedside. She made the new environment hers. Her fingertips and palms hurt as she chipped, and droplets of blood wept into the cotton. She placed the chisel down and gradually unwrapped the bandages, allowing the air to heal them.

Her mother opened the door and Delia lowered her hands. The statue remained perched at her bedside, unseen, curiously watching and incomplete.

$\cdot\ \cdot\ \cdot$

The clock tower chimed, permeating through the cement hospital walls. Helen looked up. The psychiatrist sat opposite her, a few lines of hair scraped over his bare scalp. His eyes were close-set and grey. Like the last doctor, he wore spectacles and looked between their rims at her.

'We are in the process of assessing Delia,' he said, 'but it isn't an easy task. She isn't proving too receptive.'

'Can you tell me what happened, why she might have reacted that way?'

He placed two chubby hands on the table, crossing one on top of the other. 'I think,' he said, 'that Delia was suffering from sleep deprivation, tipping her into a mild psychosis.'

'Mild.' She shook her head in disbelief.

'Some cultures use sleep deprivation as a torture technique. It can play havoc with the mind. Were you aware that she hasn't been sleeping?'

'No. No, I didn't know that.'

'You mentioned that her partner died.'

'Yes. It was a huge shock.'

'Her lack of sleep, triggering psychosis, if that is indeed what she is suffering from, is likely a grief reaction.'

'But he died three years ago.'

The doctor sighed and rubbed his fingers together. Sweat had gathered under his arms and stained his shirt. 'Grief is a complicated thing and can affect people in unexpected ways.'

'How long will she be kept here?'

'We need to be certain of her diagnosis. We're exploring other options besides sleep deprivation. It may be that she has a psychotic disorder – most likely a delusional disorder.' He let the information settle before continuing, 'I would like to keep Delia for assessment. It's likely she will need to be here for up to five days, and if I have concerns about her posing a risk to herself or to others, I may need to extend her time here.' He paused. 'Like I say, we're exploring all options. These are just possibilities at this point.'

'I see.'

'People with a delusional disorder can still be very functional but focus obsessively on false beliefs and issues around identity.'

'I see.'

'Have you noticed any changes in her behaviour?'

Nausea tinkered within her stomach. 'I went to visit her, and she looked like she hadn't washed in weeks. She was unkempt, as if she'd been living outside.'

The psychiatrist nodded. 'Did she expect to see you?'

'No.'

'She has probably been showing you only what she thinks you want to see. Changes can be gradual, often going unnoticed.'

'Well, that's the thing.' She leant forward, 'I have noticed things, and I've been keeping an eye on her. A mother's intuition perhaps.'

'And . . . ?'

'And . . .' she took a deep breath, glad she finally had someone to tell, 'Delia has been visiting a man at a lake. He lives out of a tent.'

'Aha.'

'He bears an uncanny resemblance to Ben.'

'Her dead partner?'

'Yes.'

He paused as if considering, 'A namesake for the Benmore Dam do you think?'

She nodded and looked at him directly, 'Anyhow, she visits this man beside the lake, not far from the side of the road where Ben collapsed.'

His lips parted in surprise, then he pursed them and furrowed his brow.

Helen walked away from the hospital, her scarf trailing behind her. The outline of the hospital cast a dull shadow over the footpath. She looked upwards to the cement outline of the hospital and beyond to where a cloud stretched, and wondered if, for a moment, she smelt a breath of salt air. She stared back at the footpath and took note of a figure walking towards her, his head hanging down. The stance wasn't familiar but the person was. She gasped and her step quickened. As she passed by Delia's father, his head remained lowered. He'd aged considerably, become haggard. She kept walking, reluctant to turn, but when she did, she saw that he was gone.

Her heart pounded. It was strange. In all the years she'd lived in North East Valley she'd not seen him. She'd kept thinking she would but never had. And now, at a time when his daughter was undergoing psychiatric assessment, he didn't even know.

. . .

The sound of the river gurgled and the scent of the air was laced with moisture. Luke was proud of his new boots. He hadn't enjoyed spending the money though. The lottery winnings needed to last. He'd purchased some woollen socks too in an attempt to banish the cold.

He walked alongside the river, testing the boots' water resistance. The wool surrounding his toes warmed him through to his spine. He felt adapted to his surroundings, and the long freezing nights ahead did not seem so ominous, given the startling brightness of the winter morning. He watched the river recycle a journey along a familiar path, passing through etched trails.

A trout burst from the water and returned to it, playing with the current. It reminded him of breakfast. He cast a line and waited, the currents gurgling a conversation to him. Winter nestled into the environment and he welcomed it.

WINTER

8

A hawk flew above the spine of a tarred road, flying over the painted lines. The river swelled, pressing moisture against ice that clung to its edges, trying to slow it down. The air was white and sombre, shadowed in the distance as it fell away into nothingness.

Luke's bike was askew in the grass and two new boots marked the entrance to his khaki tent. A car grumbled to a stop. He peered out from inside his tent to see Jane emerge.

'Hello,' she called.

He moved the tent door aside and stood up, smiled and waved.

'I thought I'd come to see how you're getting on,' she said.

'Just fine,' he grinned. He pulled on his new boots and walked towards her. 'I'm afraid I don't have any chairs.'

'I'm happy to stand.'

He watched her awkwardly, 'On the way to see a client?'

She blushed, 'No, not today. I did have one in Kurow but she isn't well.'

Luke recalled Jane saying she might visit him but thought this a passing fancy. Their car journey had been relatively short yet they talked a lot. He'd told her about his time on the road, camping, sometimes staying in hostels when it was cold, meeting people along the way and craving to move on again.

The last few days he'd been attempting to wear in his new boots and standing beside her now he felt ungainly, as if he should be more animated with his hands and feet. He asked her whether she'd like to take a walk to assuage this urge. He also didn't want to appear unfriendly.

'Okay.' She removed her gloves and pinned them down with a stone beside his tent. 'It isn't as cold as you'd expect, is it?'

'No, I suppose not.'

They walked side by side, their breath forming clouds around their faces.

'So, what do you do for your clients?' he asked.

'Well,' she said, 'the question really is what don't I do for them.'

The sky clenched around them, darkening, becoming brooding.

'And what is that then?' he asked.

'Whatever they need,' she said.

She stood in front of him, close to the lip of the river, and unfurled her arms into the air. The pose was familiar. Her hands pointing skyward led his eye down the curve of her body. If lightning were to strike she had positioned herself a target.

. . .

Jane realised what she was doing and lowered her hands. Her shoulders turned inwards and she bowed her head, blushing.

She turned to look at Luke to see that he was looking back at her. She wrapped her arms around herself, watching her breath rise before returning to the car, her pretence of confidence lapsing. It wasn't the first time she'd wanted Luke to watch her.

The first few days of the school term had passed. On the fourth day, the bus rumbled to an idle outside the orchard where

Luke was waiting. He'd appeared a little pale. His uniform was baggy. The shorts he wore were light grey, not dark like the other boys. They were stained a green tinge in places. She'd need to take a closer look. His hair was dishevelled and dark circles had formed under his eyes.

As the bus drew to a stop at school Jane stood up quickly. He was first out of the door and she was second. Drawing confidence from somewhere within her, she strode ahead, her hips swinging. She'd made sure that she walked ahead but not too far. If he were to look up he would see her, another girl in a uniform, passing him by.

The school entrance was lined with trees. She spied a root jutting out but kept her head held high. The root connected with her foot, as planned, and she toppled forward, her knees and hands connecting with the ground, the contents of her satchel tumbling out. It had hurt, a lot. She made a pained noise and, sure enough, he came to stand beside her. The other students' giggles were blocked out by the moment.

She looked up and saw that his shorts were – as she had thought – stained by grass. Her eyes met his; they were green and shy.

'Are you alright?' he'd asked. His voice was kind.

She looked at her grazed knees and hands, the self-inflicted pain she'd created to meet him. Pebbles clung to flesh rubbed raw. 'Not really,' she winced. She brushed the stones off her knee. 'I was in a bit of a rush.'

'I noticed.'

'You did?'

He'd helped her to collect her books and pens that were strewn around the tree. 'I'm Luke,' he said. He held out his hand and she took it. The pain mixed with pleasure. 'Oh,' he said looking down, 'you're bleeding.'

Some of the blood from her fingertips framed the outlines of her nails, colouring them red like cherries. He wiped his hands on his shorts, leaving an additional stain.

She felt embarrassed but hadn't been able to resist taking his hand. 'Sorry,' she said. 'I'm –'

The bell rang, interrupting her.

'That's okay,' he'd said. 'I think you'll need some antiseptic or something for that.' He'd smiled. His green eyes smiled too. He began to walk away.

She'd walked parallel to him, which he might or might not have noticed. It stung her knees to keep up.

. . .

After their walk, Jane hung around. It didn't matter – Luke was glad of the company – but after a while, when their conversation petered out, she made her departure. She gave him her address on a piece of crinkled paper, a street on the opposite side of Kurow to Delia's cottage. He doubted he would visit but said that he would, for old times' sake. The address was prewritten in tilted letters.

As she drove off, the wheels of her car billowed up a cloud of dust. He didn't watch it leave. For a few moments, the air was tainted and he held his breath, then crawled into his tent.

Winter did not remain kind to Luke for long. Night approached. Clouds hung lank in the air, oiling the sky with smudges. Drizzle then arrived akin to ice, attempting to wash away the sky's bruises. He burrowed further into his tent. His skin was damp and he couldn't seem to warm himself properly, his sleeping bag no longer adequate. He felt as if the sky might collapse, his tent destined to wash away, leaving the soil stark. No one would know of his absence.

He slept fitfully, hiding his head beneath the sleeping bag during brief waking moments, but then having to re-emerge when his need for oxygen outweighed his need for warmth.

During the early morning, he lay awake, his body aching. It had stopped raining but the crippling chill beyond his sleeping bag remained.

The following two nights were similar. The sky opened its mouth and spat at the ground; the river rose and began to push towards the tent pegs. He thrust his hands out into the rain beyond the door of his tent, cupping them. Water gathered in his curled palms and he brought it to his lips and sucked. Hunger and tiredness gnawed at him. The sour weather hadn't allowed him many opportunities to hunt. Even on the days it hadn't been raining the inclination to hunt had left him and he felt listless. His fingers were numb and he curled them together into a ball, blowing into them. The clamour of the rain on the nylon played a relentless warning.

The river was rising too swiftly and he wasn't equipped for the cold, new boots or not. He couldn't stay here, that much was clear. He pulled the crinkled paper with its tilted scrawl from his pocket, looked at it, then refolded it and put it back. There was only one place he knew he could go, and it wasn't there.

· · ·

White frost clung to the edge of the lake, leaking spider webs of ice onto its surface, fracturing it. The webs dug beneath its skin, edging slowly inwards and crackling. Water that remained unfrozen dipped at its new edge, unsure where to cling or lap. The roadside too was frosted at its sides, making it appear thinner and precarious. A car circled the lake slowly and a face stared out, searching . . .

Helen parked behind a row of trees and stepped from the car, crisp air enveloping her. She breathed into the warmth of her scarf and the air that escaped formed clouds of mist. Not a single car passed on the lonely road. She stood staunch, defying the winter, scanning the edge of the lake. Delia had been found nearby, hands and feet bloodied. Helen searched for the person her daughter had sought and, unable to find him, breathed a sigh of relief. The homeless man and his tent were nowhere to be seen. The winter must have pushed him away. Perhaps now that he was gone Delia might recover and, little by little, let him go.

It was a relief for Helen to escape the sterile environment of the hospital. Her life encompassed a daily walk along a stark corridor, accompanied by a glimmer of hope that faded with the passing of each evening. Alongside the lake edge, where the world ebbed at her feet, she allowed a tear to emerge. Icy tentacles surrounding her, snuck in at the edges of her jacket. The naked vista, stripped bare by the cold, revealed hills that were dark and trees like bones.

She traced the area where Delia had walked, angry at the sharp rocks and stones that had caused her so much damage, and found an area where her daughter's head might have nestled, looking upwards, helpless, searching. The sky remained empty, diluted to a dour blue. Her posture was stooped, her prim stride depleted and exhausted. She raised herself tall again, became composed. The transition was an illusion.

Back at the car, the hum of the motor warmed her. She sat for a few moments before taking off, driving along the edge of the icy lake, searching, constantly searching, as Delia had.

She approached Delia's cottage. Its white paint reflected the incandescent winter light. The grass surrounding it had become overgrown and was layered with brush strokes of frost. She stepped out of the car, its door creaking, walked along the path and unlocked the front door, leaving it ajar, and made her way through the hallway to Delia's room. It remained in disarray, green and brown piles scattered about. She collected a selection of items to take to the hospital, making a heap of clothes on the duvet. It was her second trip since Delia had been there and as she collected the items she was reminded of a time when domesticity here had been different.

The scent of Oamaru dust reassured her, coating her with the familiarity of what had once been and could be one day again. Or so she hoped.

. . .

Even underneath his gloves Luke's fingers stung with cold as he cycled from Omarama back to Kurow. His pannier bags were laden and he soon felt his leg muscles burning and his knee joints complaining. Although the sky was bright, winter had become too harsh. The air that passed his lips chilled his lungs. With each push of the pedals, though, he was glad to be heading towards Delia and her cottage, where for a time he could be safe and warm.

He heard a car approaching from behind, driving too quickly, and shortly afterwards held his breath as a whoosh of movement disrupted the stillness. He didn't catch a glimpse of the driver behind the wheel. Along the journey, he marked the passing of cars like steps. One step closer. Two. A long stride. Three steps closer. Four. The brightness of the surroundings hurt his eyes and so from time to time he closed them, cycling blind. The journey was tedious and his energy waned.

Outside Delia's cottage he laid his bike on the grass, approached the door and knocked. There was no response. It hadn't occurred to him she mightn't be home. He cocked his head. Leaving his bike by Delia's cottage, he walked back towards the highway and line of stores. His body felt stiff from having leant over so long and he was pleased to straighten out for a bit. He didn't know where to go. There wasn't anywhere really.

His steps led him along a familiar path to the Four Square. The door tinkled as he entered and an old man looked at him over a pair of spectacles. Tom. Mister Tom. Bloody hell, Luke couldn't believe the old fellow was still alive.

Mister Tom winced and chuckled, 'Luke!' he said, 'it can't be.'

'It is.'

'My sight might be failing me these days, but I'd never forget your face. How the heck are you doing?'

'Good, good.'

'Keeping out of trouble, are you?'

'Of course.'

Mister Tom reached under the counter. 'A Lotto ticket,' he said, 'for old times' sake. I bet that's what you're after.'

Luke nodded.

'I heard that you'd won. What were you, a couple of weeks off eighteen?'

'Something like that.'

Mister Tom waved a ticket in the air and then smoothed it out on the counter. 'The price has gone up,' he said, 'but I guess you don't need to worry about that.'

Luke reached into his pocket, laid a couple of notes on the counter and picked up the ticket. Little did Mister Tom know that he didn't own a television and that it was unlikely he'd come back to the store to check the ticket in a week's time. He was humouring him.

The old man smiled. A tuft of his hair was poking out as if there were some sort of static in the store. 'I think this calls for a beer,' he said. 'A good excuse to close up shop.'

Luke grinned.

A couple of hours later Luke waved goodbye to Tom outside the pub. The old man's cheeks were rosy and Luke too was lightheaded. The sky was darkening and it was cold. He felt happy though, walking along. He'd enjoyed sharing beers with the local colour and unexpectedly felt pleased to be part of the community. He'd always shied away from that.

The trip back to Delia's cottage passed quickly but when he approached the pathway leading up to it he realised there weren't any lights on and she still wasn't home. Again he didn't know what to do; he couldn't pitch his tent on her lawn. He ruffled the grass with his boots, wandered left, then right; then stood near the door and listened, knocked for the sake of it. He sat on her doorstep, sighing.

'Fuck,' he swore aloud to anyone who might care to listen.

He burrowed his head in his hands. It was at that point that he decided he needed to find a way inside and if she returned home, he'd explain that he had to break in because otherwise he'd freeze.

She might get a shock – she might even be afraid – but he'd have to risk that.

He stood and walked around the side of the house. The studio window was ajar. He stood on a tree root and hoisted himself up, and while pushing the window further ajar, he slithered his way into the studio. He half fell to the floor, then looked around the murky room.

A few days passed. Then, from the studio, Luke heard a car pull into the driveway and assumed Delia was finally returning home. He went to greet her but when he glanced out of the window saw an older woman approaching, her stride swift. He held his breath and his pulse began to quicken. Thankfully she didn't look up.

She opened the front door without knocking and began to potter around inside. He froze, listening to doors open and close, drawers rifled through. The studio had become his temporary home and he looked around, distressed. He'd laden the ground with his camping mat and various paraphernalia. His belongings were strewn. If this woman opened the studio door he'd be caught.

When he'd first arrived, he felt like an intruder but after a time he made himself at home and started to enjoy occupying the cottage. He assumed Delia was at markets selling her statues. His breath started to ache in his lungs, making him dizzy as the woman continued to fossick in the adjoining rooms. He wondered who it was. Delia's mother? A family friend? He released his breath slowly, his fingers clasped.

She didn't linger, though the ticking of the clock seemed to pause as he waited. He heard her footsteps in the hallway, the door click shut. He looked out of the window once more. The woman's decisive stride had slowed. She carried a backpack full of Delia's belongings, opened the door to her car and got in. He glimpsed her face side on and saw she looked weary.

As the car rumbled to life and she drove away, he allowed himself to breathe properly again but knew something was wrong. Delia was gone and someone had come to collect some of her things. A woman with a key; a woman who knew her.

Another two days went by and still Delia did not return home. Luke didn't go out often, in case the neighbours noticed. Small towns are self-aware like that. People keep tabs on who comes and goes. Although he knew Delia wouldn't mind him being here, others might think it strange. He'd kept the lights off and hid his belongings behind a rearranged row of statues, dreading the possibility of the woman arriving back, finding him there, calling the police. He was, after all, trespassing.

He showered at night to avoid soap scent wafting across the street and into the noses of those who mowed their lawns nearby. He hoped the pitter-patter of water wouldn't be noticed by locals who slept. He listened to her neighbours go about their business, attending to their gardens and children. The heart of Kurow chattered. He felt claustrophobic. The town had become too large for him.

Curiously, a part of him longed for the orchard, trees surrounding and isolating him, hiding him as he was attempting to hide now. That night when dusk fell, he left the cottage, keeping the studio window ajar, awaiting his return. The orchard wasn't far. He felt a tinge of nerves. The gravel road leading to the orchard remained as he'd left it, one that he'd once wanted to use as his escape route. Bright winter stars shimmered between the trees. His boots crunched loudly against the stones.

He approached the house. Light emitted from beneath the doorway, and a shadow moved across a nearby curtain. Luke stood at the entrance and knocked.

After a few moments, he heard heavy footsteps, a clomping noise he was familiar with. His father opened the door. His broad-shouldered figure stood in the doorway, staring out into the dimness. The expression on his face was unreadable. Then his father, who he had once been so afraid of, took a step forward and hugged him.

Luke lingered and after a few moments, pulled away.

'C'mon through,' his father said.

A familiar clock ticked in the kitchen. The décor remained identical to how it had been, reminding him of the tinkle of eggs in a pot, awkward silences and the brew of black coffee. Routine was ingrained in him. Trees around the orchard murmured, spreading word of his arrival.

Alfred switched on the kettle. The water in it began to stir, disturbed. It slowly frothed and bubbled. He poured two cups of coffee, not asking if Luke would like milk. The taste was bitter and Luke disliked it but it warmed him.

Cold moisture had permeated the house. He wrapped his fingers around the cup, noticing that salt-and-pepper greys had begun to smatter the stubble on his father's face. The stains on Luke's fingers had faded but Alfred's hands remained dyed red. The callouses surrounding his fingertips were prominent.

'I can't stay long,' Luke told him.

His father looked him up and down, frowning. 'I didn't think so.' He lowered his cup. 'Where are you staying?'

'Not far.'

'Anyone expecting you?'

'No.'

'So you could stay a night then. It's cold outside.'

'We'll see.'

Luke glanced around the kitchen, pretending to take in the details. A muslin cloth covered the outline of long object propped in the corner. His eyes passed over it and then back to it. The butt of what looked like a gun poked out where the muslin had splayed sideways at its edge.

His thoughts didn't have time to linger. His fingers latched together. He was ready to visit but couldn't bear to stay.

His father stood abruptly, his mood altered. He leant over the sink and breathed heavily, the rush of air coming out in what could be construed as panic. 'I'm going to have to sell the orchard.'

Luke stopped enjoying the warmth of his cup. His bones ached.

'I'm getting too old,' Alfred continued.

'Can't you hire someone?'

'With what? All the profits?'

Luke stood and poured the remainder of his coffee down the sink. It made a dark path to the plughole. 'You know,' he said quietly, 'all of my childhood you made me work, expecting that one day I'd take over.'

Outside rain began to patter. Large droplets fell onto the branches and eased their way down, creating striated paths towards the roots.

'I was always the only one.'

'Well, no.' His father lowered his gaze. 'There was your mother but after she was gone everything changed.'

A lump formed in his throat, and for a moment he thought he heard footsteps outside the window, squelching through the dampened leaves and rainfall.

Luke told his father that he would come again, that he would help a few days each week until the orchard was sold. The offer was feeble compared to what was really wanted of him. He waved Alfred a temporary farewell, holding his hand in the air. His feet trailed through the night, this time reluctantly. He felt the weight of responsibility and guilt on his shoulders.

The sky had calmed but the earth was wet underfoot. The trees drank, sucking moisture upwards into their jaded limbs, storing it for a time when it would not be so abundant.

Having arrived back at the cottage Luke rifled through Delia's kitchen cupboards. Their surfaces were fast becoming bare. He found a tin of spaghetti and wound its top off. The little sausages inside appealed to him but the spaghetti did not. However, he wasn't in a position to be fussy. He heated the meal in a pot on the element, watching it simmer, and held the handle of the pot, took a fork and ate directly from it. His lips became lined with sauce, blood red in the dark. He filled the pot with water and placed it in the sink.

A couple of weeks had passed now and Delia still hadn't come home. One day, she would surely be back. He showered, letting the chill of the night rinse off him. The cottage was far too luxurious. His hair gleamed and his skin was clean; his stomach was full. He dried himself off, standing naked in front of the mirror. Winter was trapping him here but, strangely, he didn't mind. Steam rose off his body and stuck to the ceiling, creating a drizzle of condensation. Some of it snuck out of the window and met the night air.

He pulled on a pair of threadbare briefs and ruffled his hair, jumbling it into half-dry messiness. A gown hung over a hook.

He took it and put it on, feeling the drying warmth of its fluffy material against his skin. It was a woman's gown but that didn't matter; no one would see him. He was utterly alone with a cottage to himself.

Luke walked through the hallway to the studio. Fine dust greeted him. He'd kept the window open for ventilation and the studio was too cold. His sleeping bag and mat were tucked behind a row of statues but the prospect of the hard floor did not seem appealing. Perhaps, for one night only, he could sleep in a bed, relish the soft mattress, spread a duvet over his body. He was clean. Delia wouldn't notice.

He left the studio and opened the only door he had never opened, the one to her bedroom. The room was shadowy, his eyes though, had adjusted to night-time living. His only light whilst camping, besides a lantern for reading, had been the light of the moon and stars. The lights in the cottage he kept off to hide his presence from the neighbours.

Clothes were in piles surrounding the bed. The duvet was pulled back and an imprint of where Delia had slept remained. A wide-brimmed sunhat hung over the mirror of her dresser. He didn't wish to disturb the outline so, when he crawled in, he lay in the same spot, as if she lay there too on top of him, or beneath him. He closed his eyes, content.

9

Delia followed people in white and blue. Another walked beside her and one behind her, along a corridor and down a lift. Their sneakers made an unpleasant melody of squeaks against the vinyl. Neon lights buzzed an eerie high-pitched noise, audible only to those who listened.

These people took her outside to the hospital car park where two remained to accompany her. She kept still, doing as they asked without choice or complaint. The air was moist and heavy; tiny droplets began to lick at their faces. They ushered her inside a minivan, sat on either side of her and slid the door shut. The minivan beeped as it reversed, edging its way out of the hospital gates, through the city of Dunedin and onward to Wakari, the psychiatric ward.

The journey was uneventful. Delia watched through her window, glad to see a scene beyond the hospital walls. She observed residents wandering the streets, unrestricted. Winter had settled and people were wrapped in scarves and coats, bracing themselves against bitter drizzle. Students roved the streets too. They wore an assortment of stripy hats and mismatched garb. The sky was the colour of concrete.

The bus took a path through the Octagon and upwards past Fortune Theatre to Roslyn, then lurched up another hill. Children walked past to a sign painted in what looked like calligraphy ink

– Saint Mary's School – that marked the entrance to a steep row of steps. The children didn't pay attention to the bus passing by. Their mouths moved as they giggled and chattered, like a chorus of ventriloquists in a circus announcing her departure. The bus window framed their performance.

She tried to savour the details in her memory, their little figures passing in bunches and trails, and retained a selection of images to hold. Her hands were clammy. She held her fingers clasped together. Nerves rustled through her and nausea rose from her stomach to layer her throat with bile. She leant her head between her knees and moaned.

'Are you alright Delia?' a person in blue asked. 'We're nearly there.'

She didn't respond.

The minivan approached a line of macrocarpas. A hospital loomed against an overcast sky. It too was grey, covered in mould spores, reminiscent of a previous era. An array of eyes peered through its windows at the arrival of the van, warning her to run. Its wheels rumbled against the gravel outside. A new prisoner had arrived, sporting invisible shackles.

They led her inside through a maze and left her in a room, not too dissimilar to the last but shared with someone else.

The other occupant looked up at her, intruded upon, twiddling her thumbs and fingers in an agitated way. Her flesh spread out over the duvet. She appeared masculine, wide-shouldered and ample. Her attentions were cast outside the window as she reclined back onto the head of her bed.

'This is Mavis,' she heard a voice say from behind her. 'I'm sure you'll get on just fine.' She felt a hand on her arm. 'Will see you soon Delia.'

Delia made the decision not to be intimidated by her. She placed her scant belongings on the floor. The bag made a slight thud and her roommate turned slowly in her direction.

'You can't put that there,' Mavis said with deep-throated alarm. 'There are germs.'

'Oh.' Delia hoisted her bag and placed it on the bed instead.

'And I wouldn't sleep there either if I was you.'

'Why not?'

'Because they'll move you to another room, that's why.'

Delia sighed. Mavis glared at her between two thick eyebrows, then the brows lowered, pulling her cheekbones forward. She seemed menacing but also amusing because of her garish features. One hand reached forward onto the bed and she started to pull her stocky figure upwards. She heaved and grunted to her feet.

Delia backed into the corner towards the door, her footsteps scraping on the vinyl. Mavis stepped nearer to her with reverberating clomps, stopping so close that Delia could see the woman's skin flaking away from her chin and the prominent pores of her nose.

'Don't . . .' Delia began.

She felt Mavis's breath on her face, warm and acrid.

'Are you afraid?' Mavis snickered, 'I was just going to get some disinfectant, because you soiled the floor.'

She pushed past and the door latched behind her. A musty smell lingered where she had been.

Minutes slipped by and Mavis didn't arrive back. Delia relaxed a little. The room could easily be a prison cell, except bars didn't cover the windowpane. It was her only remaining viewpoint to an interaction with the outside world, this one lonely square.

She stood by it and raised her head, defiant to circumstance. She found herself high above the car park, above rows of other hapless patients tending to their boredom. Muffled voices flowed upwards from these rooms below. She welcomed them, a quell to her solitude. She watched the clouds make their gradual journey across the sky. The scenery didn't speak to her much of a personality, unlike Aviemore. It wasn't friendly and the sky was bleak.

Her peculiar roommate didn't return until evening and she didn't carry any disinfectant. Her mood had changed. She flounced into the room, her physicality mysteriously no longer a struggle. Delia sat on her allocated bed and the woman reclaimed her spot by the window.

'Saw you coming,' she said, smiling.

Delia realised Mavis was one of the many pairs of eyes staring at her.

'Another one, joining the fray.'

'Aha,' Delia sighed, 'but not by choice.'

Mavis cackled. 'It never is, dear, it never is.' The word *dear* didn't seem to fit.

'Been here long?' Delia asked.

Mavis's smile faded. She continued to gaze out of the window and took such a long time to respond that Delia wondered if she hadn't heard.

'It's hard to say,' she said. 'It gets boring.'

'Yes,' Delia sighed.

'I wanted to do some embroidery but they wouldn't let me have any needles.'

'Embroidery.' Delia nearly giggled. 'Oh.'

'So they gave me a book instead.' Mavis moved away from the window pane, sat on her bed and reached under her pillow, animated again, and pulled out a tattered novel. Her calloused fingers rubbed over its cover.

Delia feigned interest. 'What's it about?'

'A nomad.'

Delia started to pay attention. She curled her knees up towards her body and rocked back and forth. 'A what?' Her roommate was scaring her again.

'A nomad.'

'From Lake Aviemore?'

'Why do you ask?'

Delia began to cry, tears warm against her flushed cheeks. Her body shook.

Mavis placed the book back underneath her pillow. 'You really are a nutter then,' she said. 'At least they should hook me up with someone sane.'

'I am sane,' Delia declared, defiant through the blur.

'We all think we are but we're not. I mean, you think you are but you're not, and I think I am and I am,' she cackled. 'Get that? All the bloody thanks I get, stickin' me with you.'

Mavis looked at her directly, her fingers still agitated but her face resolute. 'It's a conspiracy to keep me here,' she said smoothly. 'And now if you don't mind, bugger off, would you – I've got some embroidery to do.'

She began to stab the air, her fingers and wide outline dwarfing invisible needles and strands of coloured cotton. Her movements were precise. She held the needle between her thumb and forefinger, staring at the space intently, weaving it through miniature holes, creating a picture that only she could see.

Delia quickly became accustomed to the psychiatric ward routine. Patients were awakened early each day, given medication in plastic containers and fed meals and snacks at appointed times. A psychiatrist and a social worker were assigned to her. Another social worker led a daily group therapy session, to which she seldom contributed much. She was expected to take part in crafts but did so half-heartedly. She longed for her studio, a chisel and a mallet in her hands. Her mother visited frequently but no one else. They had to meet in a day room for visitors, the Whanau Room which sported bitter coffee facilities and gumboot tea.

She began to explore a little. The ward was relatively dull and quiet. There was the occasional outburst but otherwise an air of calm presided about the place. She discovered an enclosed patio not far from the Whanau Room with a few limp looking plants strewn in its corner. If she tilted her head at the right angle, straining her neck, she could see clouds and birds playing amongst them.

She listened to the nurses rustle efficiently about their business. Their voices were calm and lulling. She found a corny selection of romance novels plus a pile of magazines, their pages littered with every movement of the royal family. She learned about the fashion faux pas of various celebrities and on which particular private holidays they should not have worn their bikinis. Placing a magazine down, she stood to wander the corridor. The door to the Whanau Room was slightly ajar, and sitting facing away from the doorway towards the window, sat her mother. The woman began to turn her head and Delia stepped out of sight. It was strange, her mother was supposed to have left hours ago. This was an odd parallel – she herself had been staring out of the window of the patio only a minute or so ago. Her mother was shadowing her, though in a weird sort of way she felt reassured.

Despite her subdued demeanour and reluctance to talk about her supposed problems, she was allowed to walk outside for half an hour each afternoon, accompanied by a group and a counsellor. She circled mindlessly on a thin path near the designated smoking area, although the smoke chafed her lungs and those smoking stared past her. The days were long and boring. The people known as professionals irritated her with the questions they bombarded and probed her with. Sometimes she concocted what she thought they'd like to hear.

In the ward, Delia kept to herself too. Those who were depressed slept all day anyhow, chock-full of medication, the world around them muted. It seemed odd that she must cohabitate with these people. They needed help. They benefited from this monotonous routine. She did not. She craved to escape from it.

Sometimes she watched as the nurses worked with the patients. They were professional and kind, but she wondered if they seemed just a little afraid of their patients too. It was to do with a sort of distance that they kept. And if so, they were afraid of her too. She couldn't understand why.

∫∫∫

Delia's geography teacher, Mrs Herbert, marked the roll as the students loaded onto the bus. She was a rather bulbous woman with a cheery disposition.

The students bickered, negotiating their seating places. The loud, bombastic ones sauntered to the back. Delia sat down near the centre and stared out the window. It was smudged with fingerprints. Excited giggles and chattering escalated.

A surly looking bus driver loaded their baggage into an underneath compartment, his forehead perspiring. He thudded into the bus and slumped behind the wheel, looking over his nose at the students through a rear-vision mirror. He brushed a few lines of his hair back over the shiny top of his balding scalp. The bus lumbered out of the schoolyard.

Another teacher stood and addressed them. Delia couldn't remember her name. Mrs Kenny, perhaps, or Kenith. She usually taught intermediate students. The woman struggled to maintain her balance and leant on the first row of seats. She held her nose haughtily in the air. The class kept chattering.

'Eyes and ears towards the front,' the teacher said.

They turned their attention to her, amused. Their voices petered out. She waited for quiet before launching into a predictable burble.

'Logan Park High School,' she began in her smooth teacher voice, 'has a long-established relationship with Glenorchy Lodge. It is owned by East Otago High School, our sister school, and we're very fortunate to use the facilities once per year. You'll each need to show utmost respect so that we can leave the house in an immaculate condition.' She stood taller, the bus now on a straight road. 'We have many exciting activities in store for you. You'll be lucky enough to take part in archery and rifle shooting, as well as a challenging hike.'

A few groans emerged.

'I expect you'll all give these activities your best and make the most of these unique opportunities.'

The students were clearly starting to become bored but she didn't seem to notice. Her proud voice was drowned out somewhat by the hum.

'We'll stop along the way for a lunch break and it will be important that you meet back at the bus at the stipulated time.

You're representing the school and so you must maintain politeness at all times. When we arrive there will be chores to establish. This may include toilet duty for some of you,' she chuckled, 'something I'm sure the majority of you won't be familiar with. We'll need to stick to the schedule for the trip to run smoothly.'

The students stared at her blankly.

'If you're well behaved and the camp is a success, you may be lucky enough to take part in a disco at the end.'

Delia saw, through the reflection of the rear-vision mirror, that the bus driver smirked a little.

'So, let's have a jolly good time.'

A boy at the back snickered.

'I need to see Gerome and Don when we arrive to discuss dietary requirements. Additionally, both Mrs Herbert and I are trained in first aid, should we stumble across any problems. We hope that you'll all enjoy your time.'

Her spiel accomplished, she sat down, nodding at Mrs Herbert who was perched grinning importantly at the front.

Delia sat in one of many rows of lines in the grass waiting her turn. The sun was shining brightly and teenage voices around her rose and fell in excited giggles and anticipation. One by one they were required to kneel in the grass and shoot at the target. It was a fair distance away and reminded her of a road vanishing into the distance. The trick, they'd been told, was to align the two lines of sight, aiming for the red centre. The first line of sight was a V shape cradling the second close to the nose of the gun. They'd practised shooting blanks and were now allocated five bullets each.

The line of students in front of her began, the rattle of bullets momentarily breaking the chatter of those behind them. Their initial attempts weren't too successful. A few landed around the target on the outskirts of the circle but most pattered into the dirt. She watched the students reload. A few pairs of hands shook.

When it was her turn, she loaded the bullet and lay in the grass as she'd been taught, like a stalker eyeing her prey. Grass tickled her underbelly and its scent was calming. It was freshly mown and flat. She furrowed her eyebrows in concentration. Her sight blurred at first but then became clear. Her finger was sticky on the trigger. She took her time, visualising a line of taut string leading to the target. She squinted against the angle of the sun and her eyes watered with the pain of it. She blinked, her concentration momentarily disturbed.

She repositioned the line of string leading over the top of the gun, and when she was certain it was accurate, pulled the trigger. Even with earplugs the sound was loud, close to her ear. The volley from the others had sounded a gentle rattle in comparison. The bullet struck the target in the centre. So, too, did her remaining four bullets.

The sweet scent of the grass was blocked by a smoky aroma and the teenagers behind her were silenced.

∫∫∫

Jane left Kurow and drove in the direction of Dunedin. She arrived over the top of Pine Hill towards late afternoon. The city spread before her. Low clouds hung over rooftops, drooping condensation below.

As she passed by the university the smatterings of people walking the streets were sparse. Some students sheltered themselves in layers of coats whilst a few brave farm boys wore just Stubbies and jerseys. The boys' collars were raised. They

143

seemed ill-adjusted to city life, castaway from their parents and homely sheep flocks. They wore woollen socks but she imagined their legs were spread with goose bumps.

Jane tapped her fingernails on the wheel. She stopped at an eclectic costume shop and created, within a few minutes' perusal, what she thought would be a convincing disguise. The shop was bright and garish, full of a hoarded concoction of costumes and plastic paraphernalia. She relished the opportunity to shed her skin and become another, though the transformation was a necessity. The saleswoman passed her the curious selection of items in a tied plastic bag and smiled. Jane returned to her car, the bag rustling.

She clipped her hair back so tightly it pulled at the corners of her forehead. The wig she placed over it was black and elegant, yet uncomfortable. She brushed her lashes with mascara and curved the edges into a tightened line with an eye pencil. Her fingers shook as she struggled to position the coloured contacts. She had never used them before and the process of touching her eyes took a few attempts.

Meanwhile, cars ambled by. An elderly woman walked along the street, dragging her right foot and carrying an assortment of plastic bags. A chubby man, working his way out of a hangover or possibly entering one, sat on a park bench, his legs spread-eagled. An empty bottle lay by his feet. She shivered a little in nervous anticipation and turned the ignition. Wakari Hospital wasn't too far. She'd drive slowly.

Jane strode through the hospital corridor wearing her disguise. She bypassed the nurses' station, following the directions she'd received on the voice message, and arrived at the Whanau Room overlooking the car park. Her fingertips shook faintly and she clasped her hands. The room, although jutting out into the open air, felt claustrophobic and dim.

Delia's mother tapped at her cup. Her face was drawn and tired but when she looked up, her eyes widened. 'Thank you for coming,' she said, looking at her with a quizzical expression. 'I see you've gone to a lot of trouble.'

'Yes, I have, but I'll help if I can.' Her new black hair fell down around the sides of her face and itched her scalp. She felt foolish. It was odd she'd become so invested in the situation – she wasn't close to Delia's mother, or Delia really for that matter. The visit added a little flair to her otherwise quiet life.

'You're quite safe, you know.'

Jane noted that the woman's cup was empty and perhaps had been for some time. She took it gently from her hands and refilled it. 'Well,' she said, 'better safe than sorry. I'll admit, Wakari seems a strange place to invite me to. We could have met at a café you know.'

'Oh. I'm here so often you see. I like to be nearby, to know that she's all right.'

'You're sure I'm not in any danger?'

Delia's mother's hands shook slightly as she sipped at the tea. 'Delia, isn't like herself. It's as if the medication makes her inhuman, almost blank. She isn't a risk to you.' The chair squeaked slightly as she adjusted her position. 'I'm so sorry she reacted to you the way she did.'

'That's not your fault.'

'I hate to think what she was hallucinating about. It's an awfully scary thought, don't you think?'

Jane crossed her legs. Her wig itched. 'It was scary alright,' she said. 'Anyhow, she'll come right, won't she?'

'I believe she already has.' The mother paused. 'And to be honest, that is part of the reason I asked you here.' She stared out from the hospital patio and down at the car park below.

'And why is that?'

There was an awkward silence. 'My daughter seems to have had every treatment available.'

'Yes?'

'And . . . well, I was thinking there really is only one way to know if it has worked.' She looked intent. 'I think you should meet with her again.'

Jane raised her head in surprise to find the mother staring at her, treating her as a human and not an object. Solely, Jane thought, because she wants something from me, something dangerous.

'To be honest,' the mother continued, 'the psychiatrist doesn't think it's a good idea.'

'Are you trying to convince me?' Jane smiled.

'We'd need to meet with her in secret, as if it's a normal occasion.'

'It seems you have this all planned out.'

The mother ran her fingertips over the knots in her scarf. She would have been matronly if she wasn't so weathered. 'If we're successful we can show the doctors and they might let Delia out.'

'And if she attacks me again?'

'She won't.'

'But if she does?'

'Then I suppose her treatment isn't complete.'

'Surely you should trust her doctors? Don't you want the best for her, for her to be well?'

'Of course I do. But I also can't watch her like this, living but not living.' The mother lowered her stare.

. . .

Delia stood unnoticed in the doorway. Confirming what her mother had just said, her eyes were hazed and she felt floaty. She listened to them discussing her, the unexpected plot to prove her sane. She wore socks and, as the conversation continued, she slid away like an ice-skater, unheard.

She had decided to keep wearing the hospital gown, finding it somehow freeing. As she skated away it flew open from behind, the air from her movement ballooning it out and revealing her naked self for anyone who might care to look . She didn't mind. She was free, or at least she was going to be.

She simply had to be nice to the model – for now.

. . .

Jane drove to Saint Kilda and stepped out, breathing the salty air. The line of car parks was empty. She removed her wig and placed it in a nearby rubbish bin like an empty chip packet, then returned to the car and looked in the rear-vision mirror. She removed the two green coloured contacts and released each one into the gutter. A stream of discoloured water submerged them.

Her disguise was a failure. Delia's mother had recognised her straight away and Delia would have too if she'd been in the room. She should have dressed as a tomboy, a farm girl, not her twin with gothic hair. She thought herself a fool, and an obvious one at that. Had anything changed since she was a girl?

When she was young and stood in front of the mirror a plain sight reflected back at her. Just a girl, not one with any alluring features. Her hips weren't prominent, her chest didn't ping outwards, and her eyelashes weren't thick. She'd practised leaning in towards the glass, staring at the hazel of her irises. At a stretch, she'd looked a little sweet and innocent.

She pulled her hair out of its band and it fell around her face, framing her cheekbones. Was there anything so wrong with looking in the mirror? People looked at each other all the time. She'd stepped backwards and walked towards the mirror, practising her stride. As she approached she challenged her reflected self, glared, and narrowed her brows as if angry.

Dissatisfied, she'd released the stare and sat on the carpet, pulling her schoolbag towards her to take out a plastic bag containing items she'd bought. An eyeliner pencil and a bottle of nail polish, the colour of cherries. She coloured her nails with the brush. The scent wafted up her nostrils and she steadied her hands to allow each nail to dry. She'd held her spread fingers in the air, twirling them, ten newly painted cherries in a tree.

When they dried, Jane coated her eyes in a layer of kohl pencil, sweeping upwards at the corners. She looked in the mirror again, her new identity complete. She wasn't an innocent fool anymore, not like this. She wasn't insignificant.

· · ·

Mavis snored. Air rushed into her lungs and out like a sick car engine, spluttering and complaining. She wore a smock and her body was splayed out above the covers. Delia watched the rise and fall of her bosom and urged the night to descend further. The room was dim but her pupils had adjusted.

She quietly took out the bag her mother had brought for her from the cottage. It rustled and she felt alarmed, but the snoring of her unconscious companion continued, unaffected by the disturbance. She pulled a shirt from the bag and yanked at its buttons. They came off relatively easily. Strands of cotton fell around her feet.

Holding three buttons in her hand and putting these into her mouth, she took a jug of water from beside her bed, poured a glass full of water and raised it to her lips. Water swilled around with the buttons. She practised hiding them above and below her tongue, continuing to do so until her mouth was sore. She then removed the buttons one at a time, holding the collection in her palm. They each seemed to wink at her. She swallowed the water and placed the buttons beneath her pillow.

The following morning three brightly-coloured pills were presented to her in a yellow plastic cup. She tipped her head back, mingling the pills with a mouthful of water. Hoping their numbing effects would not seep from their dissolvable cases, her veins pulsed with nerves.

She pretended to swallow and expertly hid the pills beneath her tongue, behaving like a ventriloquist, her lips still during the transition. She opened her mouth to display a clear tongue to the nurse. The nurse nodded. Delia quickly manoeuvred the pills to a new location and reopened her mouth with her tongue already lifted. A line of patients awaited their daily dose and the nurse moved past her. Delia withheld a sigh of relief.

Out on the patio she sat in her usual chair. The hospital scene chattered behind her, and after a few minutes when it fell quiet, she rose and pretended to search for a magazine. She'd already read each from cover to cover, pawed at them, drenched their pages with her boredom. After checking around her, still bent over, she reached into her mouth and removed the pills. She eyed the limp plants in the corner, dug a few centimetres into the soil of the nearest one and buried them there, discovering as she dug that she was not the first to have done so. Looking down, she saw that her fingernails were dirtied now; she went to the bathroom to wash them, pretending to walk as if in a trance.

The bathroom stall was empty. She filled her palms with soap, rinsed her hands in water and scrubbed obsessively. Grains of soil turned the water brown and descended down the plughole.

Another patient opened the door and watched as Delia scrubbed. 'Afraid of germs,' she cackled.

Everyone seemed to cackle around here. Perhaps it was her roommate. Delia didn't look up. The patient went into the stall and shortly afterwards Delia was forced to listen to loud ablutions and an unpleasant smell wafted into her nostrils. She felt ill.

The day passed without fanfare. The model and her mother did not arrive. Tomorrow, she'd need to repeat the process.

Seconds stretched into minutes. Delia waited. Minutes stretched into hours. The monotony of the ward was all the more apparent now that her mind was clear. She stood by the window of her bedroom, watching to see if her mother's car approached. Her anticipation grew. The door was ajar, and visiting hour was looming. She'd dressed up for the occasion, wearing her regular clothes and not the usual hospital gown.

Her mother and the model arrived. Delia turned her head slowly, hearing them approach, having already spied the car in the car park. She pretended to be in a trance-like state, smiling sweetly, staring off whimsically into the distance. 'Hello, Mother,' she said in a cheery voice. 'I've been waiting for you.'

'Hello, Delia. It's good to see you're up and about.'

'Yes,' she said. 'I had a feeling the sun was shining today so I went to look.'

'It is, dear, it is. That's a good sign, isn't it?'

She felt her mother's arm on her shoulder.

'I've brought Jane with me. You remember her, don't you?'

'Of course I do.' She smiled, keeping her voice calm and low. 'So lovely of you to come.'

The model shuffled a little. Despite her obvious nerves, she exuded presence. Her voluptuous curves were more prominent than Delia remembered them.

'I'm glad to see you're looking well,' Jane said.

'As can be expected,' Delia sighed. 'You didn't want to meet in the dayroom today Mother?'

'A little privacy won't go astray.'

'You didn't tell them you were coming then – the two of you that is.' She could see a minivan approach. Two people in white and blue and a new patient stepped out. She observed the sad procession. 'That was me once,' she said, pointing. 'I'm not sure what you've heard, but they brought me here because I attacked an eel when I woke up.'

'Do you still believe it was an eel, Delia?' her mother asked, standing beside her, creating a block between her and the model.

'No.' Delia ran her hands through her hair, 'That would be ridiculous. It felt like I was in a dream or something.'

'So attacking an eel is all you remember, not a person?'

Delia pretended to try to remember. 'There wasn't anyone in the room,' she said slowly. 'A lot of orderlies came and they held me down; they were the only ones.'

The model exhaled.

'It's awfully stuffy in here,' Helen said. 'I'll open a window, shall I?' She lifted the latch and crisp air rushed in.

'I can see why they thought I was crazy.' Delia inhaled the smell of freedom as it wafted through the window. She looked at the model standing awkwardly apart from them. 'Don't be afraid.' Their eyes met for a second. Her voice silky, she said, 'I'm not crazy anymore.' She didn't blink.

The model looked towards the ground. She stooped to the floor and picked something up. It was a button. 'Is this yours?' she asked.

'Why, yes,' Delia said. She took it from her and turned it over in her palm. The shirt she was wearing was missing a couple of other buttons too. 'We're not allowed needles,' she explained, 'because some people . . . well, I'd hate to think.' She shook her head in disdain.

It was a few days before Delia was ready to leave. Mavis stood in front of the doorway. Her stocky figure completely blocked it, her hands and feet splayed out, creating a starfish.

'You think you're leaving,' she hissed, 'but you and I know you're just as wayward as the next person.'

Delia folded her hospital gown and placed it neatly on the bed. She began to fill her rucksack.

'How did you do it?' Mavis continued.

Delia didn't reply, simply continued to pack.

Mavis pulled the door shut, trapping her inside. This was against hospital policy. The people in white and blue would soon arrive to open it.

'If you must know,' Delia said, 'I didn't do anything. It's just time for me to go.'

'To go!' Mavis altered into a flight of panic. Her voice was high-pitched and alarmed. 'To go, to go,' she repeated, her words trailing off. 'It isn't safe out there, I know it,' she said. 'Not safe for you.'

The room closed in on them. Mavis stepped forward. She grabbed Delia with her clenching fingers. Her breath was rank. 'I'll test you then,' she breathed.

She leant forward, her eyes close enough for Delia to see the blur beneath them. Orderlies outside shook at the door handle, bursting it open. Mavis stepped backwards, twiddling the strands of her hair, smiling at them innocently.

'Against policy,' one said. 'Keep this open.'

Mavis waited for a few moments, listened for the steps of the orderlies retreat. She took hold of Delia's arms again, tightening her grip, squashing her biceps into jelly. 'Do you want to know what happens to the nomad in that book?' she asked with a glint in her eye. 'I finished reading it.'

Despite the woman's breath, Delia leant forward to challenge her, so much so that their noses were almost connected. Mavis released her grip a little.

'No,' Delia whispered. 'I'd like to find that out for myself.'

Mavis released her. She'd lost interest and went to stand beside the window. A new minivan arrived; a new recruit for the empty bed. Delia picked up her things and walked towards the door.

'He dies,' Mavis chortled. 'He's probably already dead.'

Delia gasped and lurched forward a little but stopped herself. Another attack would keep her here. She shut the door, nausea rising in her stomach.

Pairs of eyes watched her as she walked down the corridor, her departure mirroring her arrival.

. . .

Light streamed through Delia's bedroom window, shimmering across Luke's eyelids as he lay on her bed. How had his life come to this? He'd won the lottery and run away, but after a while, guilt had brought him back. His father, a grumpy old bugger alone on an orchard that he'd eventually need to sell without his son's help.

With his eyes still closed, Luke imagined himself lying in a bed of money – the scent of it distinct, like lying in cut up pieces of newspaper. Fat lot of good it had done him. Here he was, with nowhere to go. Who was this Delia anyway and would she even want to see him again? Was he bloody mad, or just doing what he did best? Following a road and now a girl, not knowing where the combination might lead?

He didn't want to open his eyes yet. There was nothing much to do here anyway, just slouch about the house and wait. Like a lottery ticket, nothing was certain; his life was based on chance.

∫∫∫

There weren't many people about. A man reclined against his ute wearing Stubbies despite the cold. He puffed on a cigarette and then ground it out in the dust with a heavy boot, opened the driver's door with a grunt and drove off.

Luke loitered about, kicking his heels. A truck filled with the scent of sheep rattled by, smelling like dried dags and wool. An old lady emerged from the Four Square and slowly made her way along the street. Some sort of receipt fluttered from her handbag. He saw it catching a puff of air and followed after it, thinking to return it to her. She hadn't noticed it had gone and continued to walk, hunched over.

Grabbing the receipt and turning it over in his palm, he noted it to be a lottery ticket. He started to walk after her, calling but she didn't respond and turned a corner. Rushing to catch up with her he found the street she had turned into was empty. The old lady must have been a ghost, or part deaf.

The thought was convenient. He was sure the ticket was intended for him. If she hadn't vanished, he would have returned it to her. Or at least he told himself that.

The town creaked around him, empty still except for the odd farmer passing him by. His father had sent him for milk and bread and he'd been glad for the excuse of a change of scenery. He folded the ticket and placed it in his pocket. The moment of greed passed.

He bought the supplies and procrastinated in the town for a little longer, scuffing the asphalt, visiting the local library, absorbing himself in fictitious locations beyond the orchard. At some point he returned home, awaiting nightfall to check the lottery numbers.

He held the ticket in his hand. Alone in the lounge, he could hear a light snoring coming from the bedroom opposite. The television burbled in front of him, then the lottery's trademark lyrics began. Anticipation brewed in him.

The first ball popped through the chute and a number was read out. He inched forward, keeping the volume low. The commentators blathered away. The one in the dress flounced around. He scanned his ticket, circling success with a pencil, and then, accompanied by a grin, the second. Time slowed. His knuckles were clenched around his pencil.

The third number matched. It was happening. He breathed rapidly and stood to pace the room but sat back down, staring at the screen. The commentators talked about the weather in Alexandra and Luke became impatient, urging them on through their script. The gentle snoring in the background continued its lazy beat.

A fourth number matched. He looked away from the ticket and back to it, checking his eyes weren't tricking him. And then he did the same again. He had to keep still and quiet but his hand shook and his brain cells danced in all directions. His heart rate increased to a clamour.

He held the pencil poised for the fifth number and when it was read out, the room became a surreal melting place and began to swirl. His nervousness meant it was difficult to lower the pencil to the page. The sixth number didn't match but he didn't care. He had won second division, likely around twenty grand.

His mind raced. This was his escape, or at least the beginnings of it. He could go anywhere; do anything. His hands continued to shake. In his room he placed the ticket carefully beneath the folds of the nomad book. For now it must remain a secret. He would need to make plans, conserve it.

He edged his way outside, into the crisp winter air. He ran into the darkness until the trees swallowed him – into the belly of the orchard where sound was absorbed by trees. There, alone, he began to holler his ecstasy.

∫∫∫

The air outside the cottage was stale, syrupy with clouds. Smoke emerged from chimneys, gathering into a haze. The outline of the mountains cast the cottage under a jagged shadow.

Luke was tired of keeping hidden and bored. He hadn't yet returned to help out his father as he'd promised. Something inside him held him back. He'd go next week – there wasn't any harm in letting another week slip by. Instead, he took his bike and wove his way towards the town. He cycled along the street, his fingers quickly becoming numb and a layer of chill coating his face. The stores were closed and pavements bare of footsteps. Jane's house wasn't far and he enjoyed the welcome change from the stale, lingering air of the studio.

The path was as she'd described it, sweeping in a curl beyond a tall picket fence. He lay his bike on the grass by the fence and walked along the path. The segments of the fence cast long, diagonal shadows that flickered across his eyes, the mixture of light and dark making him feel dizzy.

The maroon paint on the side of the house was chipped and peeling; the garden by contrast was neatly trimmed. He found it hard to visualise Jane manicuring the bushes into squares. The door was shaped like an arch. He rapped his knuckles on its wooden surface, the sound emerging as a weak rat-tat-tat. After a few moments, he knocked again with more vigour. Birds rustled in the trees, disturbed. The door clicked open and Jane stood in front of him, wearing a towel.

'Oh.' She blushed. 'I wasn't expecting you. Come through and I'll just get dressed.'

He followed her. A red carpet lined the hallway. He noticed that her hair wasn't wet and steam didn't linger around the bathroom entrance as they passed it. The towel was short and her long limbs were olive against the red of the carpet.

'Were you going to shower?' he asked her. 'I can wait.'

She turned, her hair flicking from her back to her collarbone. 'Would you mind?' she said. 'I've just returned from Dunedin. It's been a long day.'

'Not at all,' he said, following her into the lounge. He dropped onto a couch.

The towel slipped further down her back, revealing the line of her spine. As she walked away, the hallway swallowed her and he heard the shower turn on. He knew her towel would have dropped completely.

He crossed and then uncrossed his legs. The uncluttered room was lined with tongue and groove, tasteful and sparse. He leant back into the couch, feigning a relaxed stance. It wasn't particularly comfortable. In fact, it felt hard. Unlike Delia's cottage, not a single grain of dust lined the floor. Her home didn't give much away. He found it odd that she'd stayed in Kurow and hadn't left to explore. There was so much to see beyond this town.

After a few minutes the pattering of the shower ceased. He heard Jane open and close dresser drawers, sigh, and ruffle her things about. She returned to the lounge; her cheeks flushed and her limbs covered with a silky sort of material. Rivulets fell from the tips of her hair and lined her shoulders.

'It's so lovely of you to come,' she said. 'I was hoping you would.'

'It isn't far,' he said, 'and besides, what's the use of a hitchhiking friend if that person leaves, never to be seen again?'

'Yes.' The expression on her face drooped a little but then she looked up, smiling at him. 'We were a little more than that once.'

He nodded. 'You didn't pick up any hitchhikers today then? On your way back from Dunedin?'

'It isn't something I'm in the habit of.'

'I see.'

'Are you cold?' she asked. 'Should I light a fire?'

He didn't feel cold but the idea of a fire was soothing. 'Okay,' he said. 'That would be nice.'

He thought of Aviemore, Omarama, the Ahuriri River and

the fires he'd lit and sat beside there, the nights disrupted by the need to relight beacons of orange glow. He helped her to layer kindling onto newspaper and watched as the sparks took hold.

'I've missed you,' she said. 'Nobody knew where you'd gone.'

He hung his head.

The fire in the hearth soon warmed the room. It claimed a focal point. The silk Jane wore spilled around her, following the lines of her curves loosely, choosing where to cling. It was claret red just like the colour of his bike, mixed with black shadows in the darkened room. The fire brightened one side of her face into a subtle glow, her olive skin blending into the colour of the silk. God, she'd changed.

The silence was uncomfortable. Luke tapped at his leg, staring into the licking of the fire, avoiding looking sideways. He didn't wish to appear unsettled so stopped tapping, keeping his fingers and knuckles still. He made a conscious effort to become frozen, like a statue. He'd been bloody stupid to come here but it was too late now. It had become boring hanging around Delia's cottage, waiting day in and day out.

Jane rose from her perch and walked away. A lingering scent remained where she'd been. It wafted through his senses and made his knuckles tap again. He covered one hand with the other. He could hear the trickle of wine being poured into a glass, and then a pause as the bottle was lifted and poured again. It was red wine she poured. He knew that without looking.

She passed a glass to him. It was tall and the wine filled it to just below its rim. If he tilted it even slightly it might fall from the glass, splay out onto the carpet like blood, soaking in and staining it. He saw an image of himself trying to mop up the wine with his fingertips. He held out his hands and looked at them. The cherry stains from the orchard, although faded from his childhood, were still evident.

'Where are you staying at the moment?' she asked.

The licking of the flames reached towards him. 'Somewhere I shouldn't.'

She sat close, raising her glass to her lips and sipping at it. 'I can't imagine what it's like not having a home.' She paused. 'Well, I suppose I do know what it's like but not having somewhere to live, somewhere permanent.'

He took a gulp of his wine. It felt thick against his tongue, colouring the inside of his mouth.

'It's fascinating,' she said. 'I don't mean it as a criticism.'

'It's just a different way,' he said. 'It means I never feel trapped.'

She leant back. 'Do you feel trapped being here?'

'No,' he said, 'because my stay is temporary.'

The shadows behind her played between crevices.

'Is it really?' she asked.

'I can come and go.'

'Can you now?'

She took her wine, swilled it and drank a few mouthfuls in quick succession, paused for breath and then repeated the mantra. She stood, tipping the glass back for the final mouthful and refilled it.

He felt guilty. 'I didn't mean that flippantly.'

'How did you mean it then?'

'It's hard to explain.'

She smiled playfully.

'What do you mean when you say you've never had a home?' He realised it was the first time he had asked her anything really – about herself, her life.

'Pardon?'

'Before, you said you understood what it was like not to have a home.'

'I just meant, somewhere to be accepted. I was being flippant.'

'Ah.'

Jane ran her fingertips around the lip of her glass. 'What do you drink out there in the wild? Water and tea, I guess.'

'Yes, tea with powdered milk.'

'Nothing more?'

'No.'

'No wine or whisky?'

'No.'

He noticed that she'd brought the bottle of wine to the side of the couch. He swallowed a mouthful, the wine lulling him gradually into a quiet state of calm. She wasn't behaving like herself. It was like she was on show or something, someone different to how he remembered her. She'd been so innocent when they'd met at the lakeside, near to where he'd met Delia too. Jane interrupted his thoughts. 'So, when was the last time you were under the influence?'

'Drunk?' He smiled. 'I can't remember.'

She placed her hand lightly on his knee and drew a picture upwards along his thigh.

∫∫∫

Ice covered most of the lake's surface patched between strewn islands of water. Luke had been walking for an hour, making plans. He was surprised to find that he wasn't alone and noticed from afar that a girl was perched by the lakeside.

He approached and she turned at the sound of his steps. 'Hello,' he said.

She sat up a little straighter. 'Hello.'

Her voice was quiet and her shoulders turned inwards. He recognised her; she was the girl who had fallen over the tree root at school and scraped her knee. It was an odd memory and he was surprised to have remembered it after so much time.

'I'm sorry,' he said. 'We have met, I know, but I don't know your name.'

She looked surprised and her cheeks were flushed in the cold. 'It's Jane,' she said.

'Mind if I sit with you for a bit?'

'I'd like that.'

She smiled and he could tell she was nervous.

∫∫∫

Delia wound the car window down a fraction. Fresh air caressed her face and she breathed it in deeply. Her mother sat upright in the driver's seat. The stress that had lined her face was edging away but she didn't talk much.

The environment outside the hospital was busy. People flitted from one shop to the next, or gathered outside cafes. It was too much for her senses. Dunedin slipped away, drizzle covering the city in a solemn blanket.

They arrived in Kurow late. The sun had descended. The outline of her cottage, which had recently felt so far away, was within her line of sight.

'Can I come in the morning, see how you're getting on?' her mother asked, pulling on the hand brake.

'I'd like that,' Delia lied, understanding her mother's need for reassurance. She took her scant belongings from beside her feet and got out of the car.

The driver's door opened too. 'Do you need any help?'

'No, it's no trouble.' She hugged her mother and as she was released saw that Helen's eyes were wet. 'I'll be all right,' Delia said. 'More than anything I just need to sleep.'

She followed the path to her cottage, turning at the door's entrance to hold her hand in the air.

Once inside the cottage, she locked the door. The scent of Oamaru stone dust wafted towards her. She was hungry. She ventured inside her kitchen and opened the fridge. It was bare; her mother must have emptied it to save food from going off. Some fresh milk would have been nice. Tomorrow she'd need to restock.

She opened her food cupboard and to her surprise found it bare too. She ran her hand over its surface. All of the cans had vanished. She shook her head in disbelief. Perhaps it was necessary for her to return to Wakari and reacquaint herself with the psychiatric ward.

Her stomach churned, reminding her of her hunger. There were a couple of knives and forks in the sink, a washed out can of spaghetti. Beside an empty cup, sprinkles of powdered milk lined the bench. Had a homeless person taken residence in her cottage? Surely unlikely. There weren't any in Kurow. She suddenly felt afraid.

She used the bathroom, rinsed water over her face, splashed it in her eyes and wiped her hands on a towel. It was already damp. Her skin sizzled. Delia needed to search the house, see if there was further evidence of an intruder. She wanted to run outside, call her mother back, but Helen had long gone. Her heart pounded and she found it difficult to take steps.

She made her way to the studio and switched on the light.

White dust gathered in its corners. The statues had rearranged themselves, come to life and walked into a line near the window. The window itself was agape, pulling cold air into the room. Her shoulders raised. She looked at the statues and they stared back at her, stubborn, like soldiers in their new linear position. Had they positioned themselves there or had the open window served as an entranceway for someone else?

She made her way towards the statues, reaching up at the open frame, tripping on a sleeping mat spread across the floor. She felt as if the mat grabbed at her foot. The belongings she found strewn on the floor were familiar. They were Luke's. She'd lain on this very mat, tucked herself into this very sleeping bag.

'Luke!' she cried, but heard no answer.

Lowering herself to the floor, she ran her fingertips over his pillow and felt underneath it for the nomad book. She grasped hold of it, confirming he'd been here, living in her cottage, eating all of her food, showering, waiting for her.

Delia ran her hand over the tattered cover. It was late and he wasn't here, so where was he? Searching for her, that must be where he was. He would be worried, continually searching – as she had at the lake.

She looked at the scattered belongings again, not quite able to believe it. He'd returned for her, to live with her, to be with her. She placed the book carefully beneath his pillow, ran back through the house and opened the front door, scanning the street from left to right. It was empty. She breathed heavily, panting almost.

She left the door ajar and returned to the belly of the cottage, to where his things were, to where she could be reminded that he had been.

She would not sleep until he returned.

Luke took his bike from the grass and heaved himself onto it. His temples stung in the morning light and his stomach churned with the acidic remnants of red wine. The bike wobbled as he zigzagged towards the cottage. Kurow looked blurred and unearthly, as if it were gyrating in milk.

He dropped his bike in the grass below the studio window, not caring to hide it, and clambered inside. Wide eyes met his. Delia! The stare stung him in surprise, pierced his pupils in an instant.

Simultaneously a car drove into the driveway and she gasped, then rushed to him. 'Quick,' she said, 'you have to hide.'

She pulled him behind the row of statues and pushed him downwards. She ran her fingers through his hair and turned on her heels, closing the door. He swayed and curled to lower his head.

He heard footsteps along the path. A tap-tap on the door. He thought of his bike resting in the grass, drawing attention to his whereabouts. Somebody strode into the cottage.

'I'll put the kettle on,' he heard.

It wasn't Delia speaking, but the visitor – a woman. The same woman who had rummaged around before.

'Did you sleep well?'

'Yes.'

'Gosh, darling, you actually look terrible. Are you sure you slept?'

'Of course. I've only just gotten up, that's all.'

He heard a kettle start to rumble.

'Your social worker will arrive later.'

Social worker? God, what was happening here? The situation was fraught. He needed to hide his bike. It was unlikely the woman would come into the studio but the bike she'd probably see as she left. Adept at climbing trees silently, he clambered out the window in the same manner, like the skink from his childhood blending into his surroundings. His feet fell into the grass with a soft patter. His vision was still blurred, as if taking part in a surreal dream.

He pulled the bike to a nearby row of bushes, its wheels squeaking. He squatted beside it, hidden, waiting. The temperature was crisp. He wrapped his arms around himself and pulled his socks up, then coiled into a ball and rocked back and forth. His breath formed shapes in front of his face, twisting upwards and around him.

He began to feel terribly nauseous, the acid in his mouth tasting like bile. His mind had cleared somewhat though and he realised he didn't want Delia to reacquaint with him properly like this. She would smell that he had been drinking and ask him where he had been. He hadn't expected she'd be back. As his breath curved a haze around his face he formulated a plan to go back to Jane's house, shower and make himself presentable, then return.

He stood hurriedly, forgetting the need for silence and pulled his bike up from the grass. He walked swiftly with it past the studio window and cast himself onto it. Although he didn't hear it, at the same time the front door of the cottage opened and the woman stepped out. He was cycling away when a shrill voice pierced the air and he turned to see her rushing towards him, a long scarf trailing behind her. She had surprising speed.

He slowed and allowed her to catch up. It was too late — she had seen him, so there was no point trying to evade her.

'You!' She grasped hold of him. 'Who do you think you are, coming here?'

He reared back, alarmed. 'I was just cycling by. I don't know who you think I am.'

'Stay away from my daughter,' she hissed.

She was so close he could see the lines in her skin, the intent in her eyes. The background surroundings were blurred but in the doorway he could see Delia, who was running towards them. A neighbour peered through her window, breathing an opaque blush on the glass.

Delia's mother leant inwards and paused. 'A drunk, are you?' she whispered. 'Just stay away.'

He wrenched free from her. Delia was an arm's length away from them, coming into focus.

'Mother,' she cried, 'what on earth are you doing?' Her voice was drenched with alarm.

'I'm sorry, Delia,' he said, 'but I have to go.'

He rode along the street without looking back. Delia tried to follow him, emitting a guttural sort of wail. The woman he now knew to be her mother held her back, pinning her writhing limbs to her torso with protective strength.

He cycled around the corner and vomited a stream of blood-red wine into the gutter.

• • •

Delia pushed against her mother's arms, calling him back, her voice filled with anguish until Luke cycled out of sight. Her mother then released her grip and Delia brushed herself off as if nothing had happened.

'Why would you do that?' Delia cried.

Helen started to walk away from her, pulling her car keys from her pocket. 'There's no point trying to talk rationally about this with you,' she said.

'Rationally? Do you call berating a stranger on the street rational?'

'He wasn't just any stranger though, was he?' Her mother turned her head. 'Clearly I've made a huge mistake. You're going to need to return to the hospital.'

She opened the car door and stepped inside abruptly before turning to look at her again. 'I can't believe it, Delia, I really can't. I've spent my life trying to keep you away from your alcoholic father, and now . . .'

She closed behind the door and drove off.

Delia stood on the footpath, stunned, then ran into the cottage. It wasn't safe here anymore, just as her roommate at the hospital had warned. She would need to leave the cottage and somehow find Luke. They'd have to brave the winter in his tent, living as two vagrants. The psychiatric ward wasn't allowed to claim her again. She went to the studio and stood still a few moments as if trying to etch it into her memory. She ran her hands over the rows of antique tools.

She rearranged the line of statues Luke had created to hide his belongings and began to gather the items into a pile. The tent she found propped in the corner. She then made her way to her bedroom and hastily threw together a bag full of clothes and, returning to the studio, added these to the pile. She thought to add foodstuffs but remembered the cupboards were bare.

The front door remained ajar. She took her car key from its hook and set about transferring the pile of items to her car's boot. It soon filled. Compared to a cottage full of things, her material possessions were now scant. She had begun to cut the shackles of conventional life.

She returned to the cottage one final time, breathed in the Oamaru stone aroma at its entrance, and gently closed the door, clicking it shut. She left no note.

Her car spluttered, taking a few moments to remember how to come to life. She allowed it to hum gently in the driveway, farewelling the white outline of the cottage, then eased the gearstick into reverse. She surmised that two events would occur. A social worker would arrive and find the cottage empty. A plan would be formulated for her capture.

Also, at some stage Luke would return through the studio window and find his things gone. He would know where to find her. She drove towards Aviemore. The sky was wide and untarnished by clouds.

She parked the car near the spot she'd been found searching for him. This time she knew she'd find him, that he'd ride his claret bike along the empty stretch of gravel towards her.

She opened the car door and sat on a rock, tracing the outline of the lake in an arch with her finger. Her hands shook slightly with cold and anticipation. She didn't mind. She welcomed the cold. It had formed a union with her freedom.

. . .

When Jane opened the door, she had a stunned expression on her face. Her features were less defined and her skin pale.

'Ah,' she said, 'it's you. Couldn't stay away, then. It was rather strange of you to take off like that.'

'Well . . .' Luke shook his head, bedraggled. Nausea made his head cloudy. 'I need your help.'

'My help.'

'I can't look like this where I'm staying and maybe I can't even stay there any longer,' he babbled. 'She can't . . .'

'She can't what? Who is *she*?' Jane still held her fingers over the door handle. She moved it gently forward as if ready to close it.

'Can you just let me in?' he asked.

She opened it and he walked past her into the bathroom and shut the door. He turned on the shower and let the sound of the water cover the sound of his heaving. He brought up nothing more than a slimy trickle of red that formed a line down the white porcelain of the sink. Turning on the tap, he tried to clear the line with his fingers, smudging it. Eventually it rubbed clear.

The shower was set to cold so he twisted the dial, stripped himself bare and stepped underneath the water, leaning against the wall. He let his body sink, water rushing over the top of his head and pushing his hair over his face. It warmed his skin. He sat indulgently for a few minutes, allowing the water to cleanse him. He got out of the shower, dripping water, and searched for a towel. In a cupboard, he found a new toothbrush, still conveniently in its packet. He brushed his teeth. The white mint paste coloured pink as it mixed with red wine between his teeth.

When he finally emerged, redressed, Jane was waiting for him.

'What was all that about?' she asked. 'You could have just asked, you know.'

'I'm sorry,' he sighed. 'I'm a bit rough.'

She began to walk away from him. 'I've made us some coffee,' she said.

The aroma drifted towards him. He didn't like coffee – it reminded him of his childhood, but in this instance he thought it better to accept. She led him through to the lounge, where the previous night they had sat by the fire. That was his last clear memory of the evening, except a jilted image of Jane removing the silk straps from her shoulders, or perhaps he had dreamt that. She wasn't wearing the silk any longer, she wore a gown.

He sat on the couch in the same place that had led him to trouble last night. The fireplace was now lined with black and grey ash. She held out a cup for him. The black liquid inside was pungent and thick. He sipped at it, finding the taste surprisingly more pleasant than he had remembered it to be. A liquid layer lined his tongue.

'Coffee is the best thing for a hangover,' she said. 'I know you usually drink tea, but that won't take the edge off.'

She sat beside him. Her makeup from the previous night formed shadows under her eyes. She looked less like an actor primed for the stage and more human – endearing even, like she had been once.

'Where are you staying?' she asked.

'I . . .'

'Do you have anywhere to stay?'

'I met a woman at the lake.'

'Lake Aviemore.'

'Yes, and I've been staying at her cottage.'

'I see.'

'Except the cottage has been empty, so I've just been there alone.'

Jane sat forward, staring into her cup like a fortune-teller. Her breathing had altered and he realised she was upset.

'The cottage is near here,' he continued. 'I needed a place to hide out for the winter.'

Her breathing relaxed. 'So, you were simply staying there because you needed a place to stay?'

'Not exactly.'

She put her coffee onto the floor and ran her fingers through her hair. It reminded him of Delia having just done the same to him before she went off to waylay her mother.

'Where did you say the cottage was?' she asked.

'I didn't.'

She turned her head slowly to face him. The blackened circles beneath her eyes made her appear ghost-like and drawn. 'Is it full of statues?' she asked. 'Is the cottage full of statues?'

He looked at her and saw her pupils widen. 'Yes,' he said, the hangover swirling with his confusion, 'it is.'

. . .

Jane waited a few moments after he'd left and then followed in his direction along the footpath. The wheels of his bike left no trail through the dust but she knew where he was going. She kept herself hidden, flitting in and out between trees and lampposts, her voyeurism shadowing a familiar routine.

He didn't ride quickly, ambling along as if admiring the scenery. Or perhaps he rode slowly to procrastinate. She caught glimpses of him, a silhouette in the distance.

The cottage wasn't far. The foliage that grew around it had increased, clenching it in a spindly noose. She saw him clamber through the studio window, as she had once done. She remembered the statue of a man meditating and knew now that person had been him. He must have been visiting Delia for some time. He was the person that the delusional Delia had thought was her partner. It worried Jane that he was in the grips of a woman who'd been out of touch with reality. Possibly still was.

She made her way to the studio window and sat near to it, hidden by a tree. The air was drenched in a permeating sort of cold that left her shivering. She was nervous, listening and hearing nothing. If Delia were home, he would be talking to her by now.

She heard him rustling about but nothing more. A few moments later she saw him re-emerge from the window's mouth and clamber back out, looking flustered. His cheeks were flushed and his movements quick. Something was wrong. He lifted his bike from the grass and began to cycle once more. She instinctively knew where he would go and where Delia must be too. A sense of dread fell over her.

As he cycled around the corner, again beyond her reach, another car pulled into the driveway, one she didn't recognise. A woman stepped out, accompanied by Delia's mother. Jane heard a knock at the door, then another, and a flurry of talking edged with confusion.

Jane listened for a while and snuck away. She thought back to a time during a summer long ago when she had never been happier. Now something inside her had broken and become raw. It had been at the lake. She'd waded into the water, running her hands through it and watched the colours of the droplets reflecting light as they fell. Luke had dived beneath the surface of pale water and she felt a tug at her feet, toppling her sideways and pulling her under. When they emerged he pulled her to him, leant towards her and kissed her. A flicker of electricity warmed her skin against the chill of the water. She'd turned, coy, smiling, and looked out to the opposite side of the lake. There were rows of figures there, silhouetted black against the surface. One was tall and another stooped, a third like a person astride a horse. After a few moments she realised that the figures weren't moving. They were pylons emerging from the water, maybe from an old jetty that had since been worn away. There was someone standing there though, amongst the stumped pylons looking across the lake back at her. The person was a woman, that much she could tell, but her face was too far away to make out.

Later they'd sat at the water's edge drying off. He'd approached her at the same spot during winter and each change of season mimicked her growing happiness.

'Jane.'

'Yeah?'

'I'm leaving. I can't stay here.'

An old feeling crept back.

10

The winter landscape at Aviemore was a different character to the ones Delia had met in summer and autumn. The thin blanket of snow blended with a white sky, rendering outlines indistinguishable. Ice crunched beneath her boots, spreading cracks and shards. The seconds, leading into minutes, were excruciating. Her fingers had become numb and her nails, when she pressed against them, didn't spring back with colour. She no longer welcomed the cold.

Her body stiff, she walked towards the lake, reminiscing about a warmer day when she'd walked into the water wearing a sundress. The hues of the scene had been bright then, yellow ochre and piercing blue. The edge of the lake tickled her boots. If she were to paint a scene on a flattened stone now it would be different. The colours would veer towards pastel, influenced by the winter-white glow that surrounded her. The lake had a unique scent to it.

She searched amongst the stones by her feet and selected a flattened one. It was an empty canvas, a worn surface. She squatted and lowered the stone into the water. The submersion changed its tint from off-white to mottled opal and the sting of the chill pained her. Colours and shadows flitted around it beneath the surface. Her hand emerged, dripping onto the ice. She shivered, the stark cold of the lake lingering in the moisture that coated her skin. Her fingertips vibrating against the backdrop of pale water had lost colour. How daft that she'd forgotten to pack gloves. She layered stones to form a cairn to pass the time.

The sound of Luke's bike was a welcome relief. It parted the stones, creaking. She ran to him and stood opposite him by the roadside. At first neither spoke. They became two statues the winter had frozen into place. His pupils stirred away from her towards the cairn. It was as if they had stepped back in time, except now the stones weren't coated in sunshine.

He eased himself off his bike, crinkling the ice, stepped forward and brushed his fingertips over her cheek. The touch came as a surprise in the chill, a moment of warmth, as if even though he had truly arrived she hadn't quite brought herself to believe it. She pressed herself against his chest, moulding her body into his. It was the same temperature as his fingertips and she could hear his pulse. Winter gathered them together.

'We have to go,' she said gently. 'We can't stay here.'

He didn't ask questions, just agreed with a nod.

She pushed back from him. 'And we have to hurry,' she said, swiftly walking back to the car.

He followed her and she opened the boot, revealing the array of his things piled up.

'You've clearly thought this through,' he said, 'but where will I put my bike?'

'I thought we might be able to fit it in,' she said, then realised this wasn't possible. 'I don't have a rack.'

'I can see that.' He gave an empty laugh. 'I guess we'll have to leave it behind.' He lowered the bike into the grass, its chipped claret paint and rust seeming to shimmer. She almost wondered if he might cry. He didn't, but the glumness that coated his face became a little hardened, like water to ice.

'Material possessions come and go,' she said.

'Yes.' He was looking at her. 'I possibly taught you that.' He paused and cleared his throat. 'Delia,' he said, 'you realise that if we leave now we'll always be on the move.'

'I know.'

'You won't be able to sculpt. You'll be cast loose from all you know.'

Delia rearranged some items in the boot, uncovering as she did so a chisel and a mallet. 'There were some things I couldn't leave behind.'

She opened the passenger door for him and he stepped inside. As she sank into the driver's seat he asked, 'Any ideas where we should head?'

'I don't know. Does it matter?'

'How much petrol have you got?'

'Not much.'

He pulled a bill from his pocket and waved it in the air.

'Where'd you get that?'

'Maybe I won Lotto,' he said.

The bill hung in the air for a moment, then he pushed it back into his pocket. Delia's fingernails tapped on the steering wheel. 'I'm starting to wonder if you're not joking about that.' She sparked the ignition and the car's motor started to hum and vibrate. It didn't sound healthy.

. . .

A car pulled up beside the lake, one door flung open, then the other. Helen stepped out first and ran towards the lake edge, stumbling as she did so. A flicker of pain ran through her leg but she ignored it. The air was laden with chill. A granule of snow fell on her face. She strained her eyes, trying to find Delia, a khaki tent, or the homeless man who resided here. She found none. The snow cast the lakeside into an eerie white.

The social worker's glasses had fogged up and she took them off to rub with her sleeve. Helen couldn't stand still and began to pace along the edge of the lake as if her daughter might suddenly emerge from within its depths.

The social worker placed a hand on her shoulder. 'We'll find her,' she said. 'Don't worry.' Their breath curled above them. 'You're certain she's continuing to have delusions?'

'Positive.'

'Then we'll need to call the police.'

'This man at the lake though, he could be anyone. He could have kidnapped her.'

The words fell with the snowflakes on the empty expanse of ground. Some of the water at its edge was transforming into ice. Scanning the surrounds again, she saw, a few metres away, a pyramid-like cairn of layered stones. She envied the innocence of those who had the time to be lost in their reverie, not locked like her in escalating worry.

Turning on her heel, her ankle stung slightly. 'We'd better go.'

The social worker sighed and stumbled after her.

Helen returned home and walked slowly down the path. It was starting to grow dark and she was weary. As she approached the doorway the township became an icy blur. She pulled a set of keys from her pocket and wiggled one into the lock. The dark hallway greeted her, and she switched a light on before moving through it, closing the door behind her with a click. Her outline cast a shadow on the wall, bending midway on the floor as if her actual figure were stooped.

She squatted low and took a folded piece of paper from where it was wedged between two books on the bookshelf, opening it to reveal a map. There on her floor she ran her finger over the line of the road that spanned out from Kurow, as she had once done in the sand many years ago. The road led in the opposite direction too and so when she reached the edge of the map, she drew her finger backwards along the same path. The roads in each direction could only reach so far.

11

Snowflakes falling on her cheeks, Jane strode towards her home, collected her car and headed for the lake. She parked along a side road, nestling the car behind a row of trees. She needed to blend into the surroundings and become invisible. Out of the car the air was bitter. She felt disconnected, separate from her actions. In a moment or two she might find Luke and Delia, their limbs intertwined, and then consider what she would do. They might have frozen and become statues.

She had such belief she would find them that when she reached the lakeside and discovered it empty, she couldn't believe it. A hawk flew over the brink of the horizon, vanishing, leading a trail. The scene was a backdrop with no actors. Ice was taking residence and the isolation made her afraid. There was no one to perform to here.

Her search led her along the edge of the lakeside and she saw a familiar colour in the grass. The claret-red outline of a bike, covered in smatterings of rust, resting in the grass, waiting for her.

She ducked behind a bush and scanned the area. He must be here somewhere. As a minute stretched and bled into another she realised he wasn't. Delia must have kidnapped him, taken him far away, beyond his will. Or he had walked into the water, been swallowed by it, succumbing to the winter of his own accord.

A twig of the wild rosebush she was hiding behind brushed against her cheek, startling her, and she jerked her head backward. The glistening rosehip reminded her of the cherry orchard. When she took the twig between her fingers and snapped it, the red colouring became translucent.

. . .

Luke and Delia didn't get far. They drove to the Ahuriri, intending just to stretch their legs, and then stayed. They spoke little, each enjoying the proximity of the other. Luke erected the tent, a little further back from where it had been during his stay. His fingers were numb.

On their way, the Four Square had provided them with food but it was too cold to brew tea. He placed a bag of groceries inside the door of the tent and watched as snow began to coat their nylon home with a line of white. The river gurgled and sucked at the stones. They crawled inside, sitting opposite each other eating raisins and sandwiches. Something had reverted within them to being childlike and coy, as if reacquainting was akin to meeting for the first time.

'We're going to need to go far from here,' Delia said. 'They'll be after me.'

'Who are they?'

She took a deep breath. 'The psychiatric team.' Her fingers picked a raisin shakily out of its red cardboard packet. 'I'm not nuts, you know.'

He swallowed. 'You were in a psychiatric ward?'

'Yes,' she said, 'but it was only because –'

'Please,' he interrupted her, 'don't say it. I know why it was.' He turned away from her. The silence was awkward. He fidgeted with the folds in the sleeping bag and changed the subject. 'We don't need to go straight away, do we?'

'Tomorrow morning.'

'So soon?'

'I can't go back there.'

'Where?'

'To the ward.' She paused seeming to sense his discomfort. 'We'll never be far from home though,' she said, reaching under the pillow, 'because we have this.' Her hand floundered, discovering the nomad book but not the stone. She looked up, meeting his gaze. 'Where is it?' she asked.

'I left it behind,' he said, reluctant.

She sat up. 'We'll have to go back for it,' she said. 'Where is it?'

He looked through the door of the tent. The snow outside seemed to linger in the air before it fell. He knew that after he'd thrown it, the stone had pierced a path beneath the lake's surface, carving a sidelong spiral downwards. Once it hit the water it must have fallen slowly, as if time had slackened and there was no reason to hurry. Amongst others, it mirrored a temporary campsite above. As time passed a mossy substance would've encroached over it, hiding the painting and blending the stone with others, khaki green.

'It's under the water.' He looked at her. 'I had to say goodbye to you. To you, and to that place.'

She pushed past him into the open air. Her voice raised in pitch. 'You knew I was looking for you,' she said. 'You left and you didn't care.'

He followed her out of the tent. 'I had to keep on the move.'

'Bullshit,' she snapped, lurching away from him. 'Fuck you.'

'I'm sorry, Delia,' he said, keeping his distance. 'I'm sorry.

I was just trying to let go of you and the lake, and . . .' he stepped forward, 'I couldn't.'

The white sky around them feigned innocence. She faltered mid-fury. 'Surely you want to know why I was in the ward?' she asked.

He stayed clear of her. 'No,' he said, 'because I already know it was because of me.'

She looked at him, her pupils shivering with exasperation.

. . .

The stark branches of the trees at the orchard reached out and tapped at the window. Alfred looked out, seeing silver glints reflected off their limbs. The kitchen clock ticked, passed a monotonous hour. He took it from the wall and removed its battery, then placed the clock back on its hook. The room fell silent.

He sat at the kitchen table, tapping his forefinger on his knee. His hands ached. He hadn't bothered to heat the room in order to save money.

No one yet had shown interest in buying the orchard and Luke had not returned as he had promised. The orchard had been owned by Alfred's father, it was supposed to be kept in their family. The days were lonely and long, the work arduous. He held his hand awkwardly. It curled slightly, pained him. Arthritis, the doctor had said. Alfred hadn't believed him – cramp perhaps, but arthritis is what the elderly suffer from. His hair too was thinning and his stomach newly presented with a slight paunch.

The muslin that covered the gun didn't hide its outline. It called him to undress it, lift it up and place it on the table. After just a few moments looking at it he covered it again with the muslin and shivered. The snow outside wrapped around the house.

He heard a knock at the door. Surprised, he quickly put the gun into a cupboard then clomped to the door and opened it.

A woman stood there. She was startling and her cheeks were pinkened by the cold. Her hand was pressed against the door as he opened it. 'I'm ever so sorry for the intrusion,' she said, 'but I need to speak with you urgently.'

Alfred squinted at her. 'An urgent matter?' he repeated. 'I don't know who you are.'

The woman was clearly flustered, as if she had rushed down the path in a hurry. The snow was settling on the trees and the temperature bitter but he did not welcome her inside. 'I know your son,' she said, 'and I'm concerned that he has fallen into the wrong hands.'

'My son is a loner,' he said, beginning to close the door. 'I don't think he's at risk of that.'

The door was about to latch shut.

'Don't.' She wedged her hand between it and the frame. 'You may lose him.'

He looked at her, this strange woman at his door. 'I already have,' he mumbled.

'Can I come inside? It's freezing and surely you want to hear what I have to say?'

He considered this, decided after a moment that she was right and led her through to the kitchen. The clock remained locked at evening. He wondered what the time was now. He didn't beckon for her to sit but she didn't seem to notice.

She launched into a tale describing Luke's life at the lake, where he had met a sculptor named Delia, who had become obesessed by him. She described to Alfred how, when he had moved to another camping spot to get away from her, the woman searched for him until her hands and feet were bloody. That she'd been committed to a psychiatric ward but had been let out and that the woman had now lured him away.

He sat down, puzzled. It was odd that Luke had returned to stay at Lake Aviemore for so long when he'd been so desperate to get away. There could be truth to this unusual tale. 'Hold on a minute,' he said, leaning back in his chair. 'How do you know all this?'

'I was her model – the sculptor's model.'

Her physicality didn't seem to belie this statement.

'She didn't talk to me much but her mother did. I think because she wanted me to keep an eye on her. She told me that Delia's partner Ben had died of a heart attack by the side of the road by the lake, but that her daughter had met a man that looked just like him.'

'And then?'

'And then I learned that the man she was talking about was Luke. Delia, she'd started to blend the two into one.'

'What do you mean? As if her partner hadn't died? What would make you think that?'

'Maybe she thought he'd survived the heart attack but had lost oxygen to the brain and forgotten who he was. Or something. Because of the grief of it all, she was so young at the time. She made up something like that to make herself believe that Ben was still alive, but that he'd changed.'

'You knew Luke?'

'Sort of. I've always known him.'

He grunted. 'It sounds to me, lass, as if you're the one who has an obsession over him. What is it, may I ask, that you see in him?'

She paused, considering. 'I've always admired that he can separate himself from other people and be content alone. That he's always out of reach.'

Alfred stood up, walked towards the cupboard and opened it. He took out the gun and placed it on the table. The muslin fell aside. She gasped.

'Have you been following him?' he asked. 'Because it's true to say that you're not the only one who has.'

'Oh.' The look on her face was stunned. 'What do you plan to do with that?'

He ran his fingers over it. 'Nothing.'

There was silence. The woman appeared perplexed.

Alfred said, 'I followed him and I saw him shoot a rabbit.'

'So?'

'I envied him, admired him. He was not a boy any longer. He needed nothing from me to be self-sufficient. I took the gun from him.'

'Why?'

'I thought if he couldn't fend for himself then he'd come home.' Alfred covered the gun with the muslin. 'And I was wrong.' He lowered his head and silence stretched uncomfortably. 'What did you say your name was?'

'I didn't.'

'I'm Alfred,' he said.

'Jane.'

He looked up, met her gaze for a moment and then looked away.

. . .

Darkness gathered around the tent. They didn't disrupt it with torchlight; instead their pupils adjusted. The night brought with it further cold as they sought to brace against it. Inside the tent the outside world was forgotten. The temperature of their skin was warmer than their clothes and they used this as an excuse to gradually discard their layers.

They lay bare under the sleeping bag, her feet wrapped around his. She pressed into him, her probing becoming delicate and graceful. Her limbs encased him, surrounded him in a tangle. His chest rose and fell. The geometric lines of the tent formed a tight enclosure leaving no room for them to move apart. Their sweat became the temperature of bathwater, reminding Delia of a time they had danced a similar dance beneath the lake, observed only by fish.

The euphoria was fleeting. She tumbled from the intoxication of it back to reality. His chest had begun to settle but her heartbeat continued to pound. She became suddenly terrified, the sweat on her skin like a layer of glass.

'Is there any reason we can't leave tonight?'

'Delia,' he sighed, 'it's cold. We can leave first thing in the morning. I want to lie with you here.'

'What if they come for me?'

'They won't.'

She smiled in the darkness. The blood returned to flow through her veins.

'Besides,' he said, 'you're nomadic now. No one has any control over you.'

'They would force me.'

'We'll be gone first thing.' He ran his hand down the length of her hair. 'I love you,' he said.

She remained still, closing her eyes.

. . .

Delia fell asleep quickly. Her breathing became almost inaudible, covered by the gurgle of the river. Luke stayed awake, his mind straying beyond the confines of the tent to the orchard. The cherry trees were bare and submerged in darkness; his father lying alone and snoring, waking early to complete his many tasks, struggling. At times like this he felt sorry for not having given his father any of the lottery money – it would have helped a little, to get him out of debt at least. What his father really needed, though, was to be a young man again, so that he could run the orchard on his own. It wasn't fair to expect his son to fix all of his problems, or at least that was how Luke had justified the situation to himself since running away. He was overcome by an influx of guilt and closed his eyes, blocking his thoughts, but the image of the orchard haunted his dreams.

He dreamt of his mother as if she were still alive, sitting at the kitchen table with a cup of tea. She'd opened the curtains and for once the room was bright. She looked up at him, smiling, and he woke with a start. He'd only ever seen photographs of her and there were times when his subconscious tried to fill the gaps. One thing was certain, the orchard would have been a very different place had she been around. There were some things even lottery money couldn't fix. Delia remained lost in sleep, her brow relaxed. In the dim light of the early morning he could see that her skin was smooth, her hair draped over her face in disarray.

He thought of his visit to the orchard, his father treating him differently to before. He remembered each detail of their conversation and the setting, so familiar. Then – something he hadn't thought much of at the time – the outline of what might have been a gun propped in the corner, a shroud of muslin disguising it. And he made a connection. When his gun had been stolen at Omarama, he'd seen his father on the road that day.

He foraged into his memory to try to remember the outline, whether it was possible that the shape fitted. His guilt for leaving dissipated. His father was untrustworthy, dangerous even perhaps. He lay awake for an hour or so more, apprehension building in him.

He shook Delia awake. It was time they moved on, forever.

. . .

The pair packed the campsite before full daybreak. Their hands were numb as they rolled the tent and lodged it into its satchel. Delia stood for a few moments and watched as a thin semi-circle of sun emerged along the blur of horizon. They left no traces; they danced a deliberate shuffle to ruffle the stones where the tent had perched and retreated from their hideaway unseen.

Not too far from them, she imagined, along the banks of the Aviemore, two police cars had begun to scour the lake, the officers destined to find a rusted bicycle but nothing more. They'd be speaking in hushed tones, wondering whether something sinister was at play. The constable in charge of the search shaking his head uncertainly. The orchard boy at it again.

Delia couldn't farewell the Ahuriri easily. Her emotions were double-edged. Luke sat beside her but her home was falling away, and for how long, she didn't know. She saw that his knuckles on the steering wheel clung tight and she wondered whether this was because he, too, was sad or because he hadn't driven in a while, or much at all. They drove without speaking. Ice crystals covered the passenger window making her claustrophobic, the river's edge was a blur. Their escape should be joyous, not tinged with the adrenalin of pursuit. She closed her eyes, opening them a few minutes later as the car slowed.

A hawk lifted up off the mangled carcass of a rabbit, its beak bloody. The car passed over the carcass and the hawk returned to its source of sustenance. She watched the bird through the side passenger mirror as it faded into the distance, regal even in its scavenging.

She looked at Luke, studying the lines around his eyes and his concentration. She ran her palm along his leg and upwards to his belt. No cars passed by in either direction. The horizon stretched ahead, welcoming them.

'Where are we going?' she asked.

'We'll go to Aoraki,' he said.

Her head shook. 'We can't go there.'

'Why not?'

'It's the point of no return – there's no way out.' She looked ahead. 'The road only goes in one direction.'

'Exactly,' Luke said. 'We have to go where they won't think to look.'

The ice fringing her window's edge had begun to thaw. Mountainous tussock spread in clusters. The scene began to change and rearrange itself.

. . .

Clouds surrounding the orchard hung lank, moving inwards. Alfred could see the model, Jane, was tired. She had expended her energy ingratiating herself, spinning such a peculiar tale. He observed her long eyelashes droop as she struggled to stay awake. She wanted him to stride out into the night and search for Luke but he thought this was daft. It was too late and too cold. When morning arrived he might indulge her but he would take her with him.

He ushered her to Luke's room where she could sleep, offering a few hours' reprieve from her worries. It was a long time since another person had slept in the house. The falling snow trapped them inside, a reluctant elderly man with the beginnings of arthritis and a glamorous stranger. She seemed harmless enough – verging on obsessive but with good intentions. He pitied her a little as he gently closed the bedroom door behind her.

. . .

Inside the room, Jane ran her fingers over the bedspread. She was indeed tired but also affected by the surreal effect of having entered Luke's room. It was just as he had left it. She had so often wondered what his life had been like inside this home, but the stark surroundings of the room gave little away. The only thing that did speak to his personality was a bookshelf, empty save a row of ten or so books. She scanned the titles. There were a couple of the classics. *The Faraway Tree. The Lion the Witch and the Wardrobe.* Others she didn't recognise. She picked one up and wiped away the dust that lined its top. It was called *Mountain Shadow* and there was an exotic logo on the front. For a few minutes she stood beside the bookshelf, reading some of the words he had read, then placed the book back in the space where she had pulled it from.

Turning, she noticed that the pillow was indented and must have been for a lengthy period of time – since his departure. The sheets likely hadn't been changed. She felt it an ode to history and didn't wish to disturb it. She found a woollen blanket folded on a chair and picked it up, spreading it over herself as she lay on the floor beside the bed, curling into a ball. She shivered a little at first but then fell quickly to sleep.

In the morning, she arose early, the sharp aroma of coffee piercing her senses, and brushed herself off. She folded the blanket and placed it back on the chair. A long mirror stood in the corner. She looked into it, studying her reflection. The person who stared back at her did not remind her of herself. She imagined Luke as a teenager standing in front of it, sporting a second-hand uniform complete with grass-stained shorts.

She left the room, taking one last look at it as she did so, and made her way to the kitchen. Luke's father, Alfred, stood by the stove. He lowered an egg into a bubbling froth of water. It took a few moments for him to notice her presence. She stood awkwardly, leaning on one foot and then the other. He looked up, not because of any noise she made but because of a knock at the door.

'Here, let me do that,' she said, walking forward and taking the spoon from him.

'God, aren't I popular lately?' he exclaimed, clomping past her to the front door. 'Dennis!' he said. 'What brings you here on this fine morning?'

She remembered Dennis was the name of the local constable.

'Well . . .' The constable's voice was protracted. 'Can I come in? It's about Luke.'

'Of course it is. Come on through.'

The constable was clearly surprised to see Jane standing over the eggs, steam from the pot coating her lashes with condensation. 'You've got company,' he said, hiding an approving smirk, 'I am sorry.'

'Family friend,' Alfred grunted. 'If you're here to tell me that the boy's missing, I already know.'

The constable gave him a quizzical look. 'You do?'

'He's been gone for years – though it really don't make too much of a difference whether he's here or there.'

'Unless this time he's gone too far.' The constable paused. 'Done a runner with a young lady required to return for treatment at the psych ward.'

The tinkle of the eggs tapped in the background. Alfred paced, his eyes flitting from the constable to Jane. 'I don't know what you both expect me to do about it. The boy was supposed to come back to help with the orchard. I can't keep up with all of the work. It's too bloody hard. And now I'm expected to be out scaling the country looking for the selfish little blighter?'

He poured a coffee from the pot but didn't offer one to the constable or Jane. He plonked it on the table as he sat, sloshing some of the black liquid over his hand.

'No one is expecting you to hunt for him,' the constable said, 'but I had to keep you informed and thought you might have some idea where on earth he is.'

'No, I don't.' Alfred raised his coffee cup. 'But I can tell you one thing for sure. If you don't stop him, he sure as hell won't come back.'

As he sipped at the coffee, seemingly nonchalantly, his hands shook a little.

. . .

Helen parked at the lake. She'd brought with her a thermos filled with tea and wound off its cap, releasing a puff of steam. Delia had been missing for three days.

She sat near the cairn of stones. The precarious monument had somehow managed to remain intact and the top stone was covered in a light dusting of snow, reluctant to melt, reminding her of a mountaintop, or a volcano. She'd made the tea with milk powder and as she watched the powder intersperse with the water it made the tea cloudy, like her life – their lives. The air was bright and crisp, and the lake had a green hue. It was still. The weeping willows dangled into it and were reflected back.

After some time a ute rounded the corner. She didn't pay attention to it since Jane usually drove a car. The ute, however, stopped and Delia's model got out. A man sat in the driver's seat. She couldn't see him properly but thought he wore a stern look. She placed her empty cup by her feet and it fell sideways.

Jane walked towards her. 'Have you been here awhile?'

'Yes.'

'Well, we must hurry,' she said, urging her. 'I've brought Luke's father. I'm hoping he can help us.'

'Oh.' Helen raised her head in surprise, and then returned her gaze to the lake. She had no desire to be rushed. 'I came here early to try to see what Delia sees.' She breathed in. 'How this environment has swallowed her.'

Jane squatted down, sighing. 'And can you see it?' she asked.

'Well, it's very darn beautiful, but it doesn't move, it doesn't breathe – it's just a place.' She picked up the cup and screwed it back onto the thermos. She felt Jane's hand come to rest on her shoulder.

'It isn't just a place though, is it?' Jane said gently. 'It's a personality. Right now the lake is still but the fish move beneath it. The sky is clear but gradually clouds will play in it. Snow has fallen and then stopped. It moves, it rearranges, sometimes slowly and sometimes quickly.'

'It's driven my daughter mad,' she said, 'this place. It seduced her, drew her in.'

'And Luke too.'

'Yes.' She stood up. 'I used to blame him, you know, but I don't anymore.'

She stared defiantly at the water before turning towards the ute.

. . .

Luke's father looked out from the driver's window. He saw that the mother of the mad woman, although distraught, held a certain presence about her, a resistance to vulnerability. He wondered what the two of them were talking about as they approached the ute. Jane opened the door, ushering the ashen-faced woman inside.

'G'day,' Alfred grunted. He tucked his reddened fingertips around the steering wheel.

. . .

Aoraki's outline was adorned in thick snow and cloud hovered around its base. The road meandered, the final stretch long and curling. Other mountains rose along its flanks, light dappled between receding crevasses, some areas always in shadow, never allowed to thaw. Sharp ice faces greeted them like guardians. Unforgiving. The alpine valley floor spread before them, snow piled plentifully at the side of the road.

They pulled over and used their boots to carve a square away from the roadside for their tent. The task was tiring, the snow infused with spider webs of ice. They rammed tent pegs into the resistant earth, their fingers numb.

Delia and Luke left the tent and drove to the local pub, Heritage Inn. A group of locals turned to look at them and then looked away. The hostess ignored them and poured a pint for a punter. Her cheeks were rosy and her hips wide. The punter took his pint, sloshing a portion onto the carpet as he took a slurp. He gave a grin and a nod and joined the other locals.

The hostess poked her head into the kitchen. 'Oi, Rodge,' she hollered, 'got any more chips comin'?'

Luke picked up a tomato-sauce spattered menu. 'Hungry enough for a steak?' he asked.

Delia nodded, her stomach rumbling.

The hostess returned having overheard them. 'Hello, folks. Care for a pint with that? How'd you like the steak?'

Her attention had switched and she flashed them a homely smile, her rosy cheeks gravitating upwards.

They took their pints and made a wide berth around the locals to a table beside a fireplace. 'Better make the most of this, hey,' Delia said. 'We won't be this warm tonight.'

She thought of their tent, surrounded by a carved rectangle frame of snow and took a slurp of her pint. They'd be frozen solid by morning.

'We could stay here,' Luke said. 'Bet they have rooms for rent.'

She smiled and settled into her chair. 'We probably should save our pennies.'

'I told you,' he said, playing with her foot beneath the table, 'I can afford it.'

She withdrew her foot and looked at him flatly. Her voice was liquid smooth. 'You can't, Luke.'

'I told you, I won Lotto.'

'You did not win.' The expression on his face was perplexed. 'Winning Lotto is a bit implausible.'

His eyebrows became furrowed. 'What are you on about?'

Delia bit her tongue. A tiny droplet of blood spread around

the outskirts of her mouth, coating the insides of her lips.

'And talking about implausible,' he said, 'you don't really live off an artist's benefit, do you?'

She cast her stare towards the hearth. The blood tasted bitter. 'When Ben died I had an insurance pay out. I do get an artist's benefit though, but it isn't much.'

Her words hung emptily.

Luke looked defensive. 'The thing is,' he said, 'you know nothing about my past because you've never asked.' He raised the pint to his lips. 'But that's part of it, isn't it? You've only known me from the lake, and all the other gaps can be filled by whatever you like. Or maybe whoever you like. Am I Ben, Delia? Is that it?'

'Of course you're not.'

'Do you remember recognising me on the day we met at the lake? You knew I'd run away but you never asked why I left, maybe never even cared.'

The fire licked and purred. The locals spun tales. She listened to the fluctuating pitter patter of their voices. The air between her and Luke was punctuated with hurt.

He leant forward and spoke slowly. 'I grew up on an orchard. My mother died. My father resented me for it and I ran away.'

'Stop talking,' she said, glaring at him.

'I won Lotto, I bided my time and then I left.'

She held his stare and one moment lapsed into another.

'My name is Luke,' he said. 'Ben is the person you want me to be.'

She stood up, outraged. 'Bullshit,' she said.

She swept away, knocking the pint from the table, shards of glass shattering onto the floor and droplets of Speights hissing in the fireplace. The locals watched as she turned on her heel, stony-faced, and strode out into the cold. In the kitchen, beside boiled peas, carrots and spuds, two steaks were plonked onto mismatched plates. They were rare and leaking.

. . .

Tucked into the ute, the trio approached the Ahuriri. Jane knew they wouldn't find Luke and Delia there, too much time had passed. Perhaps, though, they had left a clue, some sort of marker pointing to their whereabouts.

The three stepped out of the ute, Alfred clomping onto the stones last. It was a seemingly inhospitable camping site. The temperature, even though the sun had established itself, was morose. Water chattered over rocks and ice crystals crinkled under their boots. The sky was oily white.

'This is where I met him,' Jane said, 'and drove him to Oamaru. He was standing here by the roadside.' She said it as if to herself; her memory elucidated. 'He must have come back here, he must have.'

Their newly formed team carved lines along the water's edge, hoping to find a dropped hat or tent peg, a piece of litter. Nothing. Their investigation was fruitless.

'How about we just drive?' Helen said. 'Drive in any direction. They can only have gone so far.'

The pair's absence was like a death. Hiding their disappointment, the team returned to the ute. Alfred drove listlessly. No one spoke. Their view of the sky above was empty, but within this barren space they garnered an unexpected companionship. There was solidity in their united goal.

They drove for hours, through Palmerston, Waikouaiti and on to

Karitane, slowing to scan and scour quiet spots. They drove until the darkening of the evening came, and then reluctantly turned back in the direction of Kurow. On another day – the following day Jane hoped – they would strike out again and not return until their task was achieved.

. . .

Driving through the night, Alfred raised his head to look in the rear-view mirror. He saw a blackened road and Delia's mother succumbed to exhaustion. Her face was framed by the dimness and her neck was wrapped in a scarf pressed into her cheek as her head fell to its side. Returning his eyes to stare ahead as she stirred, he slowed and turned into the orchard driveway. They stepped out of the ute, depleted and shivering.

'We're stupid to have driven in that direction,' Helen declared, breaking the silence. 'They wouldn't go to Dunedin, towards the hospital; they'd go inland.'

Jane shook her head. 'I think they'd go where they'd expect us not to look.'

Alfred shut the door to the ute a little too vigorously. 'They're probably not even in the bloody country,' he said.

The two women pretended to ignore that.

'We should split up, cover more ground,' Jane said.

'Tomorrow.'

Alfred shook his head and headed for the house.

'Can we stay the night?' Jane asked. 'I know it's late, but we're leaving first thing in the morning.'

He didn't nod. The two women followed him, Helen's scarf flowing behind in a trail.

. . .

Jane made her way to Luke's room, but this time she drew aside the bedcovers and crawled in. The sheets had a musty tinge to them. She ran her fingertips over the pillowslip and fell asleep.

. . .

Alfred pulled a duvet from a cupboard and placed it on the couch. Helen sat on the edge of it. Her scarf had begun to come unwound and the curve of her neck was white against the shadow.

'If you'd be more comfortable I can put some fresh sheets on my bed and you can sleep there,' Alfred said. 'I can sleep here easily.'

She smiled at him. 'That's very kind but I'll be fine on the couch.'

He fetched her a pillow and placed it on top of the duvet.

'You probably feel like this is a bit of an intrusion,' she said, 'we're hardly invited guests.'

'Well, if I'm honest I'm not used to having a full house but that's okay.'

She took the duvet and spread it out over the couch, signalling – he thought – a prompt for his departure. He stood for a moment longer in the doorframe. She removed her scarf, facing away from him. He began to retreat. It was late.

'Alfred . . .' she said, turning. 'It is Alfred, right?'

'Yes. And Helen, am I correct?' The name rolled easily over his tongue.

She nodded. 'Tell me about your son.'

They talked until the night had reached its depth. His rough façade began to fade but he could see her eyelids beginning to droop and reluctantly made his excuses.

'We've both made our mistakes,' she said, 'but does that mean we're the ones at fault?'

'No,' he lied as he started to close the door, 'it doesn't.'

He lay awake staring up at the ceiling, thinking of little yet wide awake. He thought of her scarf folded on the side of the couch, and the fact that as she slept, her neck was bare.

. . .

A trail of smoke emerged from the Heritage Inn and coiled its way upwards in a slow saunter towards the two peaks of the summit, spiralled sideways as if waylaid, then vanished.

The hostess arrived at the table with two plates in one hand and a broom in the other. Glass was still strewn on the floor and the seat opposite her maudlin customer was empty. Her rosy cheeks were less prominent and her wide hips swung a little as she sat down. 'I sent one of the boys to check on her,' she said, her eyes reassuring, 'and, mate, whatever sort of trouble you're in, you've still got to eat.' She slid the plate forward. 'Is she drunk or just . . . ah, unhinged?'

'She's drunk,' he covered for her. 'Has one too many and then –'

'Know the sort,' the hostess interrupted, leaning forward, her half-buttoned shirt revealing a copious mound of white bosom. 'I must tell you,' she said, 'when your lady friend went outside she just stood in the snow, looking out at nothing, like a statue.'

He nodded.

'Mighty odd,' she added. 'We've put her in one of the rooms to sleep it off.'

'Thank you,' said Luke. He looked down at the steak, losing his appetite and feeling foolish. 'Mind if I take this up to her?'

She pushed the second plate forward, stood up and began to sweep at the glass. 'Up the stairs, second room on the left,' she said. 'Mind if I ask one thing?'

He looked up. 'Shoot.'

'Why didn't you follow her?'

He paused, considering this, and sighed. 'Because I knew she'd come back.'

The locals he passed by were now rather inebriated. One sniggered at him, his Swanndri falling off his shoulders. The one who had nodded at him upon their arrival looked at him apologetically.

He found his way past the bar and up a series of carpeted steps, carrying the two plates. In the dark, he might have spilled some of the blood leaking from the steak but the semidarkness, plus the pre-existing stains hid this. He stood in front of the second door to the left and realised he had no knuckles to knock with. Placing a plate on the floor, he rapped on the door. Not unexpectedly Delia didn't answer.

He pushed the handle and found her curled into a ball. Her eyes were bloodshot and raw and she was refraining from looking at him. Putting their dinner plates onto a coffee table he sat on the bed beside her, gently raised his hand and stroked her hair away from her forehead. 'It's alright,' he said, 'it's alright, everything is going to be alright.'

Her eyelids clasped shut.

Luke watched Delia fall to sleep. Her cheeks were streaked with tears, and as she settled he wiped these away with a damp cloth. She was oblivious and didn't stir. The cloth moistened her cheeks, making her appear waxy like a doll. He took a strand of her hair and tucked it behind her ear. Her breathing had slowed to such a point that he could barely see her chest rise and fall.

He took a blanket from a chair and covered her. It smelt of cigarette smoke. Then he sat and watched over her, guarding her. The punters on the floor below were animated and their hollers and chortles rose upwards and seeped beneath the doorframe. For once he was glad of the presence of humanity. Locked in sleep, Delia was far away. And, he had come to realise, even when she was awake she was far away then too.

Taking his plate, he ate the steak on it, not hungry but not wanting to be wasteful either. Then venturing into the hallway, he discovered an adjourning bathroom. He tore loose strips of toilet paper, then returned to the room and covered Delia's steak with lines of white, before going to sleep.

He roused during early morning to find her awake. The plate was in her lap and she was chewing at the steak, clearly ravenous. She stopped eating once she realised he'd woken and looked at him sheepishly. An elongated, awkward pause ensued.

'I'm so sorry,' she said. 'I became confused.'

He said nothing.

'The medication they had me on at the hospital – it was pretty strong. I guess it hadn't worn off.'

He looked at her, locking his stare. 'Delia,' he said, 'do you know who I am?'

'Of course I do.'

'Because I can't be someone I'm not.'

'I know,' she said. 'I know.'

He came to her and knelt down, taking her hand. 'Do you know that I'm Luke?' he asked.

She nodded.

'Do you know that I'm not Ben?'

She nodded again, slowly. 'It isn't always this clear,' she said. 'Sometimes you are you and sometimes you're not.'

He felt her fingers tighten.

'Your faces are so similar.'

'Do you think so?'

'You know what makes me mad?' she said.

'What's that?'

'It isn't fair. Not really, accusing me. You've never asked me about my past either – about Ben, or anything. How I came to live in Kurow, why I sculpt. I'm not the only one, you know. I'm not the only one who sculpts people into versions of themselves that aren't true.'

He couldn't help but smile. 'That doesn't make any sense.'

'We've made each other into stone people.'

Her eyes were unwavering. 'You tried to sculpt me too, into someone I'm not,' she told him. 'Someone you could keep in the same place and come and go from. The only difference was that you didn't have any chisels. I won't let you do that. I'm not an ornament.'

Another tear edged its way down her cheek. He felt his body constrict and spoke with his voice low. 'I'm sorry, Delia,' he said. 'Do you think you'd be willing to give me a try? We could start from the beginning.'

She wiped her hand across her cheek. 'I want to,' she said. 'I keep trying and trying but I can't get him out of my head. It's not easy, you know – he was so like you, and now he's gone and you're here.'

Luke brushed her chin with his fingertips. 'Maybe you never will,' he said, 'and that's okay.'

She shook her head, her chest heaving and her breath quickening. 'It isn't okay. It's horrible.'

'I want to help you make things clearer,' he said, 'but I think you can only do that if you're open to it.' Her pupils were wavering, becoming wary.

She closed her eyes, her eyelids descending slowly, and he wondered if she'd heard what he'd said.

'Why don't you tell me about Ben?' he asked.

She opened her eyes, looked down at her plate and pushed the peas on it into a pile. 'Well,' she began, 'I met him at a garage sale.'

'Go on.'

'And he bought a claret-red bike.'

'Just like mine.'

'Exactly.'

'And two chipped enamel cups so we could share a cup of tea.'

Something inside him turned grey.

∫∫∫

For the second Sunday in a row Delia wandered past the garage sale, uninterested. The old lady, dwarfed by her wares, appeared odd. Her voice, as she spoke to the few sporadic local customers, rasped from years of cigarette smoking. The multitude of items had accumulated into a greater number since Delia's last morning stroll and spilled out lavishly onto the footpath.

A young man wandered between the haphazard aisles, stooping from time to time. His feet were bare. A claret bike on the footpath seemed to draw his attention.

'It was my grandson's,' Delia heard the old lady say.

The stooped woman walked towards the potential customer with surprising speed. Delia slowed her pace and listened to their conversation while pretending to fossick in a box, smiling at him beneath a wide-brimmed sunhat.

'He doesn't visit anymore,' the seller continued.

The man stood, holding the bike against his waist. 'Your grandson?' he queried.

'Yes. He rode it when he was a teenager. His feet couldn't touch the ground. It'd be perfect for you . . .'

He admired the bike. It was in good condition.

'I'll make a good price for you,' the old lady breathed, leaning her wizened face towards him.

Delia listened, keeping her eyes on the box. She found there, amongst other dusty remnants, a pair of enamel cups, seemingly unused. She held one in her palm, pretending it appealed to her.

The seller acknowledged Delia only momentarily – 'Two dollars, love,' – then returned her attention to the sale of the bicycle. Delia fumbled in her pockets, only to find one and then the other empty. She glanced around, embarrassed. The customer with the bare feet watched her, grinning. He held her in his gaze, frozen for a moment, like a pair of statues in a museum.

'I'll take the bike,' he said to the seller without taking his eyes from Delia, 'and the two cups.'

Delia felt a flush spread across her face.

The seller was surprised. 'You haven't even asked how much it is,' she exclaimed.

He reached in his pocket and handed her a bill. 'Will this do?' He swung his leg over the bar of the bike and pedalled slightly.

'One twenty,' she negotiated.

He reached in his pocket and pulled out a coin. 'One hundred and two,' he said, 'for the bike and cups.'

The old lady panted slightly but subsided. She clasped the bill to her chest, then folded it neatly in half and put it into her pocket. He placed the coin in the old woman's palm. It gleamed.

The man rode the few metres to Delia and swung his body off the bike. His straggly hair was lightened by the sun, his tanned face shadowed by a light beard. His green eyes gleamed.

'I'm Benjamin,' he said, grinning boyishly at her.

He was, in a strange sense, familiar.

∫∫∫

The twigs of a cherry tree tapped at the window, waking Jane. In her tired state the previous night she hadn't noticed that the curtains were open and now morning light streamed in. Trees outside were covered in a newly laden coating of snow, and with no breeze playing amongst them, they were still and skeleton-like.

She pulled back the covers, thinking to make herself a cup of tea and then rouse the others. As she opened the door she could hear a light snoring emitting from Alfred's bedroom, his door ajar. She thought it odd that he didn't have a mental alarm clock, waking him early each morning – maybe he did usually but the poor man was likely so exhausted from their search. It was good that he was having a break from the stress of it all. Her socks on the floorboards made delicate rustling sounds, but none so noisy as to awaken the other two. The kitchen door too was ajar and she squeezed through it, closing it gently behind her. She stood in the room for a moment, attempting to absorb an imprint of Luke's childhood. Three chairs were placed around the table, two pushed in.

She opened a cupboard in search of teabags and found only coffee. Come to think of it, Luke's father mightn't drink tea. She supposed he must have some teabags somewhere for visitors and opened each of the cupboards one by one, finding most bare. She realised as she did so that it was unlikely he had many visitors and this saddened her.

207

She opened the kitchen door once more, tilting her head to sneak a peek into the lounge, and saw the outline of Delia's mother tucked beneath a duvet, her head poking out and her eyes closed. Jane decided not to disturb them after all, returned to the room and tucked herself into bed once more. She waited patiently, a plan formulating in her mind.

The mother awoke an hour later. Jane heard her moving around, then Alfred's snoring ceased. She heard him come out and offer Helen a cup of coffee. They gave the impression of domesticity, as if happily going about their business, having forgotten the fact that their children were missing.

Jane made her way to the kitchen. 'I've been thinking,' she said, 'that it would make more sense for us to split up – cover more ground.'

'You're probably right,' Delia's mother said, 'but the truth is I wouldn't know what to do once I found them. I think we're better to search together.'

Jane wondered if she saw a smile pass across Alfred's face.

'None of us know what to do once we find them,' he said reassuringly.

'Well then,' Jane said, 'maybe it's best if you two set off together and I go alone.'

Alfred and the mother nodded. They turned to look at each other.

'Oh, the coffee,' Alfred said. 'I'd forget my head if it wasn't screwed on.'

He switched on the kettle and then opened the cupboard. He pulled out two cups and turned to Jane as if having forgotten she was there. 'Would you like one?' he asked.

'I might pass,' she said. 'Get on the road.'

Jane didn't leave Kurow straight away. She decided to take her time. Luke and Delia wouldn't keep moving, not initially. They'd be perched at some idyllic spot. Jealousy surged through her. She drove to Delia's cottage and slithered in through the studio window.

The statues stood in an eerie line, watching her as she entered. They were remnants of Delia, ghosts of her past, reflections of mental turmoil. The room's musty smell had increased. Stone dust swirled in her lungs, making her cough again and again. She withheld the urge to splutter, cautious that the neighbours might become aware that the cottage was suddenly occupied. Strange happenings had been occurring in the community and she knew they'd be alert to anything untoward.

She ventured into Delia's bedroom, seeking clues. The room was different to what she had remembered, more claustrophobic. She sat on the bed, remembering that Luke might have slept there. Grief welled in her, and she felt that her body was swollen. The walls closed around her. The breath streaming in and out of her lungs became rapid. She recognised the influx of a panic attack and lay on the bed, calming herself. Her body felt like it might convulse, sending flickers of electricity to her skin and then radiating inward towards her chest. She concentrated on stilling her breath, and after a minute or so, her heart rate settled. She curled on her side, her eyes moist.

Her impaired vision fell on a bookshelf. It was crammed full. She rubbed her eyes clear and squatted before it, scanning the titles. On the lowest shelf was what looked like a photo album. Curiosity drew her to it. It was wedged tightly between two thick books pressed by an alignment of others on either side. She pulled these sideways and yanked it free. Its cover was tattered and dusty.

She knelt on the floor and opened it, the pages splaying wide, revealing delicately glued pictures of Delia and a man. A man who wasn't Luke. He looked similar though.

In one picture he stood barefoot beside the lake, proudly holding an eel. In another he sat by a campfire, the glow of the flames reflected on his face.

She pawed at the pictures. Delia and the man astride a bicycle, Delia's hair positioned into an elegant twist and her companion beside her, his hands wrapped around her waist. On the last page a picture of the pair wrapped in winter garb, the backdrop Aoraki Mount Cook. She peeled the photograph away from its backing. It furled as the glue clung to it. She folded it neatly in half, creasing a line between the couple, and placed it in her pocket. The album she left open on the floor, remnants of disturbed glue marking where the photograph had been.

She crawled back through the studio window, a trail of dust resembling dainty snow following her.

...

Alfred prepared the coffee, tipping each mug to the side as he poured then straightening it when near full with a well-practised motion. He slid the first one forward and poured another, wrapping his hands around its edge, forgetting to hide the red stains. He was a man of few words usually, but something within him had begun to change. His gruff exterior had become a farce. He wanted to talk and not stop talking; he had so much to say.

'Do you think it's wise for us to travel separately?' she asked.

'Separately?' He'd momentarily forgotten.

'To the model.'

'Ah, yes . . . well, she'll play things her own way.'

'I guess so.'

They each took a slurp of their coffee. He saw that her scarf was wrapped around her neck again. 'You know,' he said, 'we're looking for two people who don't want to be found. In a way, they've been lost for a lot longer than this.'

'That doesn't mean we should stop looking though.'

'No.'

'Stop hoping.'

'No.'

Out of instinct he took her hand and looked up surprised, realising what he had done. Her skin felt soft beneath his and he pulled away.

'We could take a break, I suppose,' she said quietly.

'And do what?'

'You could show me the orchard.'

He found it peculiar to think of the orchard as a place for relaxation but it was, he knew, peaceful.

They donned their coats and walked into the crisp morning air. He noticed as they walked that she seemed genuinely relaxed – not like the other days when they were searching for Delia. She shed the weight of her loss with each step and appeared to walk airily. The chill teased the exposed skin on their hands and cheeks.

'How long have you lived here?' she asked.

'Always.' He rested his hand on the bark of a tree. 'Except I have to sell.'

'I see.'

'It's too much work for me now,' he said.

She placed her hand on the bark too. They walked on through the orchard in a series of disorientating twists and turns. The trees around them seemed more astute than usual, as if registering a change. He took her hand again. Her scarf came loose and brushed against his shoulder.

The day at the orchard passed swiftly. Alfred and Helen entered into a sort of daze, momentarily free to do as they liked, undisturbed below the covering of trees. Even the snow was beginning to melt away, such like that they were able to warm it with the stark contrast of their happiness compared to their regular lives. Within each other's company it was possible to block the imminence of their search and the feeling of hopelessness that accompanied it.

'I'm guessing you haven't always been alone?' he asked.

'Delia's father didn't cut it.'

'No?'

'He had some issues.'

He nodded. 'Don't we all?'

'And yourself?' she asked. 'Was Luke's mother an alcoholic too?'

'No,' he said. 'She died in childbirth.'

'God, really?'

'With Luke.'

She cast her head aside. The trees rustled slightly. The silence was jarred.

. . .

Delia and Luke went for a walk too, pleased to leave the peculiar hostess behind.

They wove their way across snow-covered schist and tussock. The ice faces that had greeted them when they'd first arrived at Aoraki glinted at them, astute guardians watching their steps. Luke's boots were waterproof but Delia's soon became moisture-laden. She traipsed on, the numbness lessening her enjoyment.

They followed a trail, weaving their way upwards in search of a vantage point. Their breathing became heavier. The cold chafed their lungs. Aoraki loomed over them, reflecting a mirror image into the lake below. The image was a disconcerting reminder of how easily life can turn upside down, but the mountainous spire itself commanded a spiritual presence and consumed them.

'Luke,' she said as they trod, 'tell me about the orchard where you grew up, before you ran away.'

'I never grew tired of the taste of cherries. And –' he smiled '– I loved finding hideways in the trees. That's where I read the nomad book and got the idea to escape.'

'Escape?' Her mind was wary with confusion. She rolled the image of the orchard over, toyed with it, kept her voice deliberately low and calm. 'To get away from your father?'

'He worked me too hard. Day in and day out picking cherries. It was too much. I wasn't able to be a kid. And my father – well, he was never happy. Never.'

'Where is he now?

'At the orchard, I expect. He barely ever leaves it, but soon he'll have to.'

'Why is that?'

She tripped on schist and steadied herself. A thought occurred to her. She was getting to know him. Asking him about his life.

'He's getting too old, and without me there to help him . . .'

'You left him!' she said, alarmed.

'Of course.'

'What do you mean, of course? You left him alone?'

'Yes.'

She became angry, suspicious. He'd left the lakeside, hadn't he? Left her. 'Do you always leave people?'

His footsteps became heavier. 'I can't stay anywhere for long.'

'He must miss you,' she said.

'Like your mother misses you,' he retorted. 'She's searching for you now, I'm sure.'

Her toes had started to ache and pulsate. 'She wants to trap me,' she said, vehement.

'Exactly, and so does my father. That's why we have to keep on the move.'

A lone hawk flew above them, searching the lower slopes where the tussock had thinned out for prey. Delia's stride and resilience against the chill had lessened. She paused at an outcrop of tussock and he waited for her. Her breath collided with his and intermingled. The mist furled upwards.

'You'll need some new boots if we're to see out the winter here,' he said.

'Yes,' she agreed, 'and socks.'

She pulled them up and the liquid between her toes squelched. A tinge of homesickness stabbed at her. It wouldn't be possible to sculpt schist, it simply wouldn't.

· · ·

The pair had remained at the pub lodgings. Their tent had spent one night alone beneath a winter sky and was now propped in the corner of their room which was strewn with other belongings. Winter had become too much. Besides, staying at the pub meant they were comparatively hidden.

During early morning Luke quietly dressed and stood by the window, admiring Aoraki framed by the rectangle of glass. Its flanks appeared sharp and inhospitable. A shaft of light hit its surface and wove its way downwards to where jagged, snow-covered rocks lined its base.

A few minutes passed and he reluctantly pulled his attention away from the window frame. Delia's boots were upside down, seeping water onto the carpet. He walked towards the pair, picked one up, checked its size. She stirred, content.

'I'm going to go and buy you some boots,' he said.

'What? And leave me here?'

'Yes. You can't go an entire winter without proper boots.'

'No.'

'And you can't go back to where we came from.'

She sat up, worried. 'What if they see the car, follow you?'

'I'll just have to be careful, won't I?' He kissed her on the cheek and pulled on his own boots. 'Don't worry, it'll be fine. What colour boots would you like?'

'Brown,' she said, smiling. 'Hiking boots should be brown.' She propped herself up. 'And Luke,' she said, 'bring us some food, would you?'

She was looking at him differently now, fondly and anew. She reclined, releasing him.

Luke drove, content. The driver's window was opened slightly and a steady stream of refreshing air washed over his face. He looked in the rear-view mirror, watching as Aoraki fell away. He rounded a bend and it dropped from his sight. He would try to be swift – journey to Oamaru, collect boots, bike equipment, replace his stolen gun and return. The task would allow him time to think. Why was it that he wasn't running away from Delia as he had with Jane? Was it because he was older? Or was it that she confused him so? Challenged him? For a while he had been someone else, someone who hadn't grown up at an orchard, won the lottery and run away.

He wanted to help Delia now, and help her get to know him as Luke, the real Luke. Maybe he didn't need to run from himself anymore – he could run with her instead. Of course it was madness, crazed, in fact, to wander around the country with someone who was so unhinged. Maybe he was unhinged too.

He hadn't wanted to follow Jane. Not even for a little while, not even now that she'd changed so much. As he gazed again in the rear-view mirror a sudden thought grabbed him. The car boot was empty now, and if he were careful, he might be able to collect his bike. It would still likely be slumped in the grass at the Ahuriri, albeit a little rustier than before. He could purchase some oil for its chain as well as the pair of boots for Delia. A bike rack might present itself too.

During the drive towards the Ahuriri his body became tinged with nerves. Electrical currents ran through him towards his skin. He contemplated whether the bike was worth the risk, but deep down, he knew it was. Surely, he told himself, he would need it again? His nerves rattled in him. The scene passing by blurred – parched grasses in emptied fields, their tips hardened with frost. The sky was a milky expanse blending with the layer of white, making each inseparable.

The gurgle of the Ahuriri River when he arrived was a welcome melody. He hadn't left forever after all. Nothing remained in a state of permanence. No cars passed on either side and the sky remained bleak and empty.

He located the bicycle nestled in the grass and pulled it up towards his hip. Its weight and feel were an extension of him. It had succumbed to less rust than he had thought it would. Smatterings of the claret colour still remained. The wheels manoeuvred reluctantly as he pushed it. He urged the rickety pair on amidst squeaks and complaints and rested it against the side of the car. He pulled the rear seatback forward and pushed it in. The angle of the metal was awkward but he managed it. He didn't dare look over his shoulder to see if anyone was watching him.

He set forth again to Oamaru, pleased to pursue a destination, the road lilting. Driving around the streets, he noticed the Oamaru stone spires, reminding him of Delia's statues. A large steampunk robot puffed fire after a young boy entered a coin into its belly. A lady in old-fashioned garb stepped out from the doorway of a café beneath a quaint Victorian Tearoom sign. Down a side street he scanned the shops on the left, swung the car around the roundabout and looked at the shops on the right, finally discovering a narrow shop front.

A bell on the door tinkled as he entered. The man at the counter looked over his glasses at him, the corner of his lip curled a little. His skin was puckered with scars and covered in an oily sheen. 'What can I do you for?' he wheezed.

'My .22 was stolen,' Luke said, 'and I need to replace it.'

'Stolen you say?' He leant forward, his breath rancid. 'I think I've got just the ticket.' He reached under the counter.

Luke put the gun in the car, covered it with a sweatshirt and locked all four doors and boot, checking each one – the central locking wasn't reliable. He went on a shopping spree, buying Delia's boots, a bike rack, bungee cord and some oil. Returning to the car he set up the rack for the bike and lifted it on. He made one final stop and drove out of Oamaru, deciding to sleep a night in the car. The return journey wasn't too long but he liked the feeling of the freedom on the road. After parking at a quiet spot alongside the coast, he wound the window down a smidgeon and lay back, covering himself with a musty old blanket.

He stared out the back passenger window at the evening sky. The lapping of waves formed a delicate background and the scent of salt gathered around his nostrils. He closed his eyes for what he thought was a moment and when he opened them was surprised to discover that night had fallen. A near full moon hung in the sky, appearing too heavy to stay afloat. He studied its face, pockmarked like the man from the store. Light pulsated silver shards. A car or two passed him by but did not pause.

Luke closed his eyes again but the moonlight was too bright to allow him an easy passage towards sleep. It pressed through the thin skin of his eyelids and shimmered opal at the edges of his lashes.

He must have slept at some point. Come early morning, when the sun crept up, it awoke him. He stepped out of the car stiff, stretched, and sat on a piece of driftwood and breathed in the salt air. After some time he retraced the road back to Delia.

He arrived back at the pub by early afternoon. Not too surprisingly Delia wasn't where he had left her. He tipped his head at the landlady.

'She's at it again, I'm afraid,' the woman said. 'Wandering around in the snow.'

He nodded and made his way outside. He found lines of footprints leading away from the entrance and back to it, stemming from many different directions. She'd carved a highway of paths in her anxiety, mostly leading in the direction of the roadside.

He felt a twinge of guilt. She would return though, he was sure of it, and sure enough, she did. She must have known he was there, somehow, because shortly afterwards he heard the approaching crunch of her waterlogged boots in the snow.

Her eyes were wide. 'Where were you?' she asked. 'I was worried. I thought they might have caught you and . . .'

'It's okay,' he said, somewhat exasperated. 'I just wanted to take my time and enjoy the trip.'

'Enjoy the trip!' she snapped. 'While I was here freaking out, wondering if I needed to hide, or rescue you somehow?'

'Come here,' he said, beckoning. 'I'm sorry. I didn't think.'

She stood stubbornly for a moment or two and then crumpled a little. 'Maybe I'm worrying too much,' she said, 'but I couldn't possibly go back there, and I can't lose you either.'

'You,' he joked, 'worry too much.' He pulled her to him. 'You'll like your new boots,' he said. 'Top of the line.'

She smiled and leant into him.

'And,' he said, 'I got you something else.'

He pulled her hand, tugging her towards the car. He untied the bungee cord from the bike rack, lifted off the bike, wheeled it aside through the snow and opened the boot. There, wedged in to the corner, was a large chunk of stone.

The proprietor watched the pair between the windowpanes, chuckling.

A light snow began to fall and clouds gathered into a coverlet, blocking light. Luke returned to the car and began to drag the rectangle of stone through the snow, leaving a path. At the pub's entrance he picked it up and carried it over the threshold. A group of hardy fellows were leaning over the bar, murmuring grunts over the tips of red noses. Their Swanndri had similar patterns to the peeling wallpaper.

The landlady narrowed her brows. 'You two settling in?' she asked.

He nodded.

'What's that for then?'

'A sculpture,' he puffed. 'One for you to place at the entrance to the pub.'

She beckoned him with her finger and he placed the lump on the carpet. 'A sculpture, you say.'

'Yes. Delia – she sculpts.'

She took a pint and sloshed it onto the bench, offering it to a punter without looking at him, her attention concentrated on Luke. 'Well,' she said, 'I can't have her ruining business, banging away.' She leant forward, her bosom wiping dust off the counter. 'Or, for that matter, ruining the carpet.'

'She'll be careful,' he said, and picked up the stone again.

'Sure you want to let her loose with chisels?' she chuckled.

He ignored her and began to stagger towards the stairwell, the smell of yeast in his nostrils, the weight of the stone painful against his finger joints.

'How long do you two plan on staying?' she called after him.

He paused mid-step.

'Because just quietly,' she said, not so quietly, 'there have been some calls.'

A succession of calloused local hands lowered their pints. Luke froze, his knuckles white, his cheeks turning the colour of the stone. He didn't turn. He heard her sigh and step away from the bar. Her musk permeated the yeast and he could feel a whiff of breath on his neck.

'I said that I hadn't seen a man and a woman with a khaki tent,' she whispered, 'and that anyone wanting to camp out here would be bloody stupid because they'd get hypothermia.'

He shivered at the thought and walked away.

Jane closed her door and the sound of it latching shut broke the silence. She walked along the pathway. The surprising breath of sun was pleasant, though she noticed clouds had begun to gather and their presence filled her with a sense of foreboding. Yet the moment she opened her gate and closed it behind her she knew she couldn't turn back.

She sat in the car for a few moments, her mind hazy. As she departed Kurow she knew that pairs of eyes watched her.

Jane ignored warnings of ice, her foot heavy on the accelerator. She drove as if on autopilot, her face locked in a scowl. In Twizel she stopped to stretch. At first the street was empty but then a man rode past her on a claret bike. She didn't see his face but from behind he looked like Luke and for a few steps she trailed after him. He turned a corner and disappeared beyond her sight. It seemed a possibility that the figure astride the bicycle may have been a figment of her imagination, or an apparition. She shivered, the chill of the town unwelcoming, and returned to her car.

Leaving Twizel, she passed a braided river, the soil chipped away in chunks. The heating in her car had stopped working and with each passing minute the chill along her spine increased, imbuing a sense of dread.

The photograph tucked in her pocket remained folded while the shadows of the hawks brushed the grass as if following her – or warning. Their eyes were sharp and pointing.

Delia and Luke did little, just enjoyed their surroundings and each other's company. They ate from the food supplies Luke had brought in Oamaru. Many hours were spent lying in the warmth of their room, drinking pints and pleasuring in the effects as Aoraki bent and swirled. They went hiking and tested Delia's boots. He'd bought her a couple of pairs of woollen socks too and she seemed chipper with the result.

'I'd like to go hunting today,' he said one morning, aware what her reaction would be.

'We have enough food, don't we?'

'Yes,' he said slowly, 'but we need to make it last.' He could tell she was beginning to sulk.

'It isn't as much fun here alone,' she said.

He leant forward and kissed her on the cheek. 'Solitude is a fantastic thing,' he said. 'You just have to learn to accept it.'

He took his new gun from underneath a pile of belongings. Bright light rushed in through the window, beckoning him out and away.

'Where will you go?' she asked.

'Not too far.'

He slipped out of the door.

. . .

Delia made her way up the stained carpet steps to their room. Taking a chisel and a mallet from her backpack, she settled herself in front of the stone, running her fingers over it. She half-heartedly chipped at it but couldn't continue. Her shoulders sagged and her head hung limp. She looked up and stared at it, a pockmarked rectangle, one she no longer had the urge to manipulate and lowered the chisel to the carpet. Later she might carve a hawk, the one they'd seen chewing on road kill.

She closed her eyes and dozed upright. A few minutes of brief reprieve. She locked her hand around the chisel and when she roused, she noticed it had dug into the carpet, drawing a line. She felt renewed vigour and picked up the chisel to carve a face in the stone, gently, a shallow relief. The face exuded only remnants of Ben's appearance – it was Luke who emerged from the stone. Delicate flakes of dust fell to the carpet and hid its stains. The face she carved was the size she could cover with the palm of her hand, looking at her directly, smiling.

'Ah, there you are,' she whispered. 'I wondered where you'd gone.'

. . .

The landlady paused mid step and listened. The irritating banging had stopped half an hour ago. The door was slightly ajar and she looked in to see the mad woman stooped over the slab of stone, her hair hanging over her face. The woman didn't stir and the landlady took a few moments to stare at her.

After a long period the woman looked up at the stone, the straggles of hair falling sideways away from her features. She must have been sleeping because she appeared to be in some sort of daze. She sat for a few moments before picking something up from the floor. The landlady couldn't see what she was doing, but she was so absorbed it would have been difficult to disturb her from the task. The woman continued to stare at the stone and smiled, then began to whisper. Something the landlady couldn't catch and, 'I wondered where you'd gone.'

The woman – Delia, the young man had called her – then continued to stare ahead, into nothing, at something only she could see. The proprietor stepped away.

She walked down the staircase and when she got to the bar poured herself a whisky, no rocks. She swigged it back, then picked up the telephone. The phone book was open at the yellow pages and she flipped through to find the number of the Dunedin Police Station. It was time – this bloody woman had the potential to ruin business.

• • •

The sky formed a semi-circle and the mountains loomed around him, drawing his eyes along the road. Luke got off his bike, lay it beside the road and began to walk, his footfalls light. A hawk looped in a circle above him and upwards through waves in the sky. It became a speck and then tilted away from the road towards Aoraki. He followed it, his footsteps making imprints in the snow.

The mountain drew him towards it and when he turned his head the roadside and pub had vanished. The air was crisp and empty, and like many times before, he felt insignificant in it. He scanned the ground carefully, pausing to see if anything moved. It didn't. The flicker of rabbits' tails eluded him.

He lowered himself onto a rock beside a cluster of wild rosehip bushes and placed his gun at his feet. The rosehips glistened translucent red like diluted blood.

• • •

Just before the pub, Jane pulled over to inspect its surrounds. She got out and stretched. The air was stinging and shrubbery obscured her view. The road faded towards Aoraki and she marvelled at its size.

She took the photograph out of her pocket and looked at the image of Delia and the man. His name was Ben – Delia's mother had told her that. The minute figure could easily be Luke's twin.

Jane held the photograph to the side of the mountain and wondered if she was right, whether he'd be here at all. The image was a little faded but the two pointed spires matched. A mirror image of the past, bereft of two lone figures that had once stood beneath it.

She liked that the line was creased between the figures and ran her finger down it, then returned the photo to her pocket.

. . .

Hours passed. Delia sat at the bar, a third pint in front of her. Her finger tapped on the glass and she stilled it quickly, feeling bored and anxious. She thought too much and each passing thought weighed like a concrete cloud, increasing her worry.

The bar lady eyed her from behind the bar. Her bosoms, Delia noted, were each larger than her head. She wondered how the woman kept her balance.

'Might be about time you spilled your story there, lass,' the bar lady said.

Delia looked up in surprise. The woman was looking at her imploringly, surprisingly caring.

'Nothing too ground-breaking.' Delia's voice slurred a little. 'I was with a guy who died of a heart attack. He was out on his morning run and just keeled over.'

The caretaker nodded, furrowing her brow.

'Except that would just be a normal story, wouldn't it?' Delia took another slurp of her beer. 'He had an affair before he died, with a model.'

'A model?'

'A life model. Except she wasn't a model back then. I've been sculpting her.'

'Why?'

'To make her into someone she's not. To hurt her without really being able to hurt her.'

'That doesn't make sense.'

'Chipping at someone you hate with chisels doesn't make sense?'

The caretaker leant forward but Delia had forgotten her. She'd tried so hard to hold on to Ben and block out what he'd done. Deified him in her memories. Pretended for so many years that she hadn't seen what she'd seen. She hadn't confronted the model, just kept sculpting her, each chip of the chisel an attempt to exorcise her anger. The anger consuming her.

'What was his name?'

'Ben.' The name rolled easily off her tongue.

Delia wished Luke would come back. She hadn't heard any shots but he probably wouldn't be allowed to hunt too near the pub, so must have gone further afield. Either that or there weren't too many rabbits around. She needed to search for him and turned to leave.

'Wait on,' the caretaker prompted. 'Something I want you to consider.'

Delia turned again, perplexed, her head cloudy. She had to find Luke.

The landlady took Delia's now empty pint glass. 'When you think about it, this Ben guy, he's kind of been lost twice.'

The floor moved beneath her, gyrating. 'What do you mean?' she asked.

'Well –' the landlady measured her words '– when he shacked up with that model of yours, that's when you really should have grieved for him, said your goodbyes.'

Delia left the pub and wove her way towards the car. She drove slowly down the driveway but once on the road, she accelerated. The beer in her veins lightened her spirits. It was finally time for her to let Ben go.

She had better things to look forward to.

. . .

Jane put the photograph in her pocket and got into her car. She took a deep breath and sparked the ignition. The car spluttered to life, a deeper-than-usual, surly rumble. Once she found Delia and Luke she would approach the pair quickly, catch them off guard, then single Luke out and show him the photograph. He would understand that it wasn't him Delia loved at all.

She pressed sharply on the accelerator, heading in the direction of Aoraki, the road twisting. Ice cliffs rose around her in jagged relief.

. . .

Delia thought of Luke as she drove. Her eyelashes were clogged with tears and her sight blurred. She reminisced about meeting him by the side of Lake Aviemore, alone as a single hawk vanished over the horizon. The cairn they'd made. The stones he'd skimmed. How meeting him, when she'd gone there to be alone, had seemed odd, like she had stepped back in time.

. . .

A car approached and pulled over. Luke stood up, leaving his gun resting in the snow. He was surprised to see Jane step out and run towards him. Her cheeks were flushed and her hands shook a little.

'I've something to tell you,' she said, her words floating like snowflakes.

He stepped backwards, suddenly alarmed. 'Please don't,' he said.

Her face fell, the shimmer of sadness glistening in her eyes. She reached into her pocket but her hand remained there. 'I –'

'Nothing happened that night we drank,' he said. 'I know that now. I've been thinking about it a lot and I stopped you. I stopped –'

'I know,' she said, 'but why would you need to stop me? You don't know how long –'

'I do,' he said. 'I've always known. You're the one. You fell and grazed your knee, maybe on purpose.'

She looked at him, shocked, her lips pursed together.

'I just . . . I'm sorry. I've always known who you are and that you used to follow me and that maybe once you even . . . ' He faltered and slowed his speech. 'I met this woman at the lake – Delia. I told you a little about her and . . .'

Jane reached into her pocket and pulled out a photograph. From where he was standing it was blurred. She pushed it towards him, holding it out. He could see that a line was creased between two figures. One was Delia, and the other, he knew, must be Ben.

'That woman, Delia,' Jane said. 'You don't know what I know. She doesn't think you are who you are.'

Luke nodded.

'She thinks you're Ben. She thinks you're this man in the photo. She's never loved you.' Jane thrust the photo at him again. 'She's insane, Luke.'

Luke walked towards her and put his hand on her arm. He could feel the warmth beneath her jacket. He then lifted his hand and brushed her cheek. 'It might be true,' he said. 'For once I don't want to walk away.'

'But you always walk away.'

'I'm tired of that.'

Jane stepped backwards. She looked beyond Luke, and suddenly held up her hands in fright.

. . .

His claret bicycle lay by the roadside. Delia scanned the surrounds but she couldn't see Luke.

She pulled the car to a halt and stepped out, her breath rising into a cloud. Her hands were cold. A trail of footsteps had been carved into the snow and she followed them, matching her footsteps to his, her head lowered. For a moment she thought she heard voices, but it couldn't be so. Her memories were haunting her again. The voices sounded like those of Luke and the model.

Then she realised the voices were real. It was Luke's voice she could hear. She raised her head and saw him. Surprised, she recognised the model standing opposite him, so she hadn't imagined hearing them after all. They were in plain view but still far in the distance. She hunkered down behind a raised mound of schist, obscured slightly by a wild rosebush.

Luke and the model were talking. The model was emotional though Delia couldn't hear what they said. The model was crying. The symmetry was overwhelming. It was happening again. Luke and the model were here together, meeting in secret just like the model had met with Ben. She felt that she might faint. And then, as her head spun and her stomach lurched, she saw it.

The gun.

It was resting in the snow, nestled there as if waiting for her. She edged towards it and picked it up. She trembled, her heart racing. The metal was chill on her fingertips. She lifted it cautiously; it was heavy. She raised her eye to stare through the sight.

At first her vision was blurred and she blinked away tears. She visualised string leading to her target, the line of sight aligning exactly. She held her breath.

The model was looking back at her.

Delia's finger hovered over the trigger, and time, for a moment, stopped. The model was crying, she realised, and objects didn't cry. Statues didn't cry. People did. She stared at her for a moment longer and lowered the gun, looking down in horror at it. Her fingers unclenched around it and she dropped it and ran through the snow, stumbling, bawling. She heard footsteps run after her. The model's; an eel slithering after her leaving a trail as it melted the snow. Grey. Muscle. Hiss.

The footsteps quickened, multiplied and she fell forwards. Her hands clutched at the bitter snow and she dragged herself up again. She didn't look back.

Delia revved the car engine. The world of alcohol and emotion swirled into a torrent. She forced herself to look ahead as if about to drive through a tunnel. It was long and thin with a flicker of light somewhere far in the distance. Her periphery blackened. Somewhere in the darkness the eel was coming towards her and she didn't know from which direction. Time slowed. She couldn't make sense of the gears. Feel them, but not see them, forgetting which came first. Her foot stumbled, heavy on the accelerator. The tunnel pulled her into it, twisting. She swerved to turn, her eyes blurring anew with tears. She drove fast, faster, the car swerving and when she was out of sight she pulled over, opened the door and vomited in the snow. Her sight cleared and as a dribble of vomit fell she looked up, white emptiness contrasted with what had been the black of the tunnel, dizzying her.

Delia wiped her mouth and then another surge came and she vomited again. The snow turning beer-yellow.

She realised she'd driven in the wrong direction – to collect her things she'd need to return to the pub. Did she even need to collect anything? She couldn't think straight, and with her body weakened, she got back in the car and turned back. If she were to see the model or Luke she would drive past and say nothing. She was done with both of them.

She closed her eyes, driving blind. When she opened them though, through the blur she saw a hawk, blood covering its beak as it tore on road kill.

When I die, I'll be a bird.

It began to lift off the ground in an awkward manner, its heavy body slowing its ascent as it lurched into the sky. *I'll fly over lakes and mountains.* She fixated on it, its stare drawing her towards it.

Another bird will fly beside me.

She swerved to miss it, and as she did so the car skidded on the gravel, hitting something. *Sometimes we'll wheel in circles just to get a closer look at the grassy hillocks and cadences of the water.* It wasn't the hawk – that had lifted itself in time above the car and swooped by close. *Everyday we'll see the curve of the earth; green, blue, opalescent skies.* She saw in the rear-view mirror that it was a rusted claret bicycle, or at least fragments of it scattered over the road, one wheel spinning forlornly. *All of this will be in silence.*

And a stationary body, one that she knew must be his.

Sweet silence.

The moment of realisation stretched and then she wailed as the car skidded to a stop. *It won't matter if we're lost.* She flung herself out of it, struggling on the surface of snow and ice. *Why?*

She neared the body and saw him slumped, his face nestled on the roadside. *You wonder . . . because the whole world will be our home, with Otago at the centre.* It had a contented look, as if he hadn't known what was coming and had simply been enjoying the ride. *With my wing tip I'll be able to touch something precious, and pure and true.* The hawk lifted up and away, casting a shadow over her stooped figure.

His mouth was open slightly. *A bird's life may be fragile but I can imagine no other life so perfect.* His face wasn't damaged.

Freedom.

She ran her hands through the snow, clutching at it, the mounds of ice his body had pressed sideways, like knuckles.

Freedom is the air beneath our wings raising our silhouettes by delicate wisps of lift that take heat from the winding roads. Delia emitted a guttural noise and lowered to the ground spreading the snow. *Freedom is the crisp texture of unpolluted surroundings.* The chill and ice clawed her. *Freedom is circling amongst these invisible columns and currents along ridges of mountains and beyond to empty spaces never before occupied and untainted by prying eyes.* Her stomach contorted and her lower back knotted.

The snow surrounding her turned the colour of cherries. Her body convulsed and weakened. She writhed in agony. It consumed her and pulsated. Aoraki swayed, swirling ominous shadows above.

A blurred face appeared, concerned and stressed. The face hovered above her. Something changed in her . . .

A flicker.

A blur.

She lurched away from Luke, towards the eel whipping around and clasping onto her, clasping tight. She clutched at her throat and wielded her with a guttural grunt onto the ground. Shadowy snakes thrashed around her. The model's eyes stared. Huge.

'Urgahhhh,' Delia cried as she squeezed.

She pressed her body into the road kill that the hawk had been chewing on, coating her face red. The model squirmed attempting to slither back into the snow. Delia tried to grab her again but the slippery skin whipped beyond her grasp. The grey blur coughed and spluttered, falling to the side, falling away. Gasping, the model's gills crying out for air.

An image of the eel at the lake, its expression in death, locked as it had been moments before in life. Its body curled on a rock. She sobbed between her breaths, lingering in the cold, until eventually her anguish like a river running still and then dry, stopped.

Expended.

Still and silent.

Empty.

The model rolled over the ice, hands flailing. She coughed. Then she raised herself from her battered state and stepped forward. Delia gasped and tried to turn, but then the model hugged her. Her body felt warm and she sank against it. Their cheeks were clammy as they pressed together. For a moment, they battled the same grief. And then Delia returned to the nomad in the snow.

• • •

The model stood back, watching, as she had always done. Resigned to this now, her body weak and bruised. Her nails torn, her face cut and weeping.

• • •

Delia rocked back and forth and then lowered her ear tilting it sideways to the space just above Luke's mouth. The hawk was high above them now and she could see it hovering in her line of site.

'Where would you like to go next?'

She paused to listen, shaking.

12

There was a sharp knock at the door. Alfred roused himself and hurriedly put on some clothes. He wondered who might be calling at such an hour. He approached the door and opened it, still in a mild state of undress.

It was the constable. There was something uneasy in his eyes and he held his policeman's hat tightly.

'Can I come in?' Dennis asked, already halfway through the door.

Alfred nodded and led him through to the kitchen.

'You'd better sit down,' the constable said, swallowing.

'I'm okay standing.'

There was a moment of silence.

'Luke was hit by a car, on his bicycle.'

Alfred stared at the constable, information seeping in. His face displayed no emotion but inside he crumpled.

'Dead?'

'No.'

'Is he going to be okay?'

'I don't know.'

He teetered as if he might fall and the constable steadied him. Alfred blinked, seeing nothing, then pushed the constable away and slumped into a chair.

Helen rushed into the kitchen.

Alfred kept a stoic look on his face. He stood up slowly and walked past them and out of the house. Under the trees his knees gave way. His shoulders shook. When eventually he stilled, his heart still pounded. He heard footsteps through the trees and looked up to see who was coming.

No one was.

The leaves rustled. In his memory the cherries fell around him in a rainfall of tears.

. . .

From inside Dunedin hospital Delia heard the Octagon clock tower chime. Her feet floated along and, like a ghost or deity, she left no indentation in the carpet. In this mind-washed way she was able to face these sterile walls and corridors with less fear. It was as if she were merely a passing visitor, swept through by chance. Her exhaustion added to an overriding belief that she was separate from this place – that she didn't belong.

The white walls gleamed and the corridor seemed to shrink. The light hue of the vinyl and the stale, trapped air were suffocating and sickening. She reached a lift and its doors silently opened as if cued for her arrival.

She was sucked upwards and her stomach churned, bile rising in her throat. The lift released her onto the twelfth floor and into an identical corridor. It smelt of new paint and disinfectant. She began to walk again, a familiar well-trodden path. She passed rooms with people bent over loved ones, people alone, people sleeping. She watched nurses attending to patients. Their uniforms were crisp and clean.

She came to a door painted the same charmless colour as the

walls. Pushing it open she placed herself in a chair. She sat as she had for many hours, stooped and depleted.

Seconds merged into minutes and those into hours. She stayed beside Luke, his breathing gentle and reassuring.

'He looks like he's dreaming.'

She turned, surprised, to see her mother entering the room, then sighed and resumed her vigil. 'I hope he's dreaming sweet things.'

'What do you hope he is dreaming about?'

'Camping at Aviemore. The sunshine on his back.'

Delia stared out towards the window. It was lineated with aluminium sills. She longed for it to open and crisp air to flow through but it was latched shut.

Her mother shuffled. 'He seems peaceful.'

At this Delia smiled. In a private delight she saw the two hawks fly in through the hospital door, their feathers catching a glint of sun through the window. Her tension lifted and she swayed a little in her chair. She raised her head towards the ceiling and noticed, absentmindedly, the whir of the fan. The birds joined in and flew above her, mixing with the circulating air.

'How long have you been here?' her mother asked.

Delia envisioned her mother in a separate reality, not noticing the hawks that disturbed the ward. Helen's reality was plain and devoid of birds and beauty. Delia thought it best to keep what she could see to herself. This proved difficult and she required all her stamina to simply sit still.

The birds began to fly more frantically, their beating wings brushing against her cheeks. They didn't seem to mean her any harm but she felt an alarming sense of claustrophobia. The white walls closed in on her again. The birds were thrashing in such a violent way that their feathers started to fall in swift circles to the ground and layer the room with down.

She turned to her mother, struggling to speak. 'A while now,' she said. Her voice quavered; her mind wary and confused. 'His eyelids fluttered earlier.' She wondered if this might be true and kept her head lowered to stop the hawks from brushing against her. She struggled to hide her distress. 'Do you think he can hear us?' she asked.

'I hope so,' her mother said.

'But do you really think so?'

'I don't know, love.'

'He's going to get better, you know.' Delia paused. 'It'll just take time, that's all. Ben was never going to get better, but Luke will, you'll see.' She looked up.

Her mother leant forward, her face appearing aged and vexed. 'Maybe you should take a walk, get some fresh air.'

'He'll know if I'm not here.'

She turned to look at her mother.

The fluttering became less frantic and alarming, the hawks now mimicking parrots becoming used to this caged existence. They settled and perched themselves regally at the edge of the bed, standing astute as two guardians over him.

'Sometimes I drift off. Feel like I separate from my body. That must be how he feels.'

Her mother exhaled with an elongated sigh. She bent over the figure between them and placed her hands around his ears to create a cocoon. 'I'm taking Delia for a walk now. Is that okay with you?' She lowered her head towards his face so that it hovered just above the contours of his mouth, as if listening. 'He says it's fine.'

Delia became as still as Oamaru stone, carved, resolute. The porous consistency of the stone, though, allowed the words to creep in at the edges of her consciousness. She kept her head stooped, defeated. 'If Luke is dreaming then I don't think he'll mind if I dream with him.'

She closed her eyes and allowed them for a moment to seal shut. The two hawks launched themselves swiftly into the air and crashed violently against the window. The glass didn't smash. The hawks fell in tandem, stunned, to the floor. The world outside wailed and called for them to join it.

Delia opened her eyes. She found herself still in the hospital room, her mother asleep in one chair and Alfred asleep in another. There was someone new in the room too. The model. Jane. She, too, sat opposite Luke; she, too, looked exhausted.

This time Delia didn't lurch forward to attack. She stayed calm. 'I saw you, Jane,' she said, 'with Ben all those years ago, swimming beside the lake.'

The model's eyes widened.

'That was you?'

'What?'

'I saw a woman across the lake, standing amongst . . .' Jane then seemed to hold her breath for a moment, shook her head and sighed. She looked up and their eyes met and held as if in that moment something clicked. 'No, it wasn't Ben you saw.'

Delia shook her head. 'Then who?'

The pieces of the puzzle fitted before Jane spoke.

'Luke.'

She thought of that day at the lake, standing amongst the pylons. The two figures far away but so familiar. The pylons by her sides like apparitions keeping guard of their secret. 'I don't understand.'

Jane was looking at her in a kind sort of a way.

'He left, like he does. Luke. He ran away.'

'He came back though.'

'Yes, and then ran away again – with you. I never thought he'd do that, never thought he'd . . .' she trailed off. 'He was always searching for something new, something that I couldn't quite grasp, and he was always on the run from the orchard and his past.'

It occurred to Delia that Jane knew a lot about Luke – more than she did. Delia didn't really know him at all. She'd left it too late to get to know him. The loss of Ben had warped Luke into someone he wasn't – not Ben exactly, but a hybrid of him. Sitting now beside the hospital bed and his still figure she understood, finally, how foolish she'd been. His chest gently rose and fell, signifying hope. 'I think he ran away with me because we both had no direction and . . . really, we both still don't, and now . . . well, he can't go anywhere and neither can I.'

Between them Luke's breath was gentle and they each, Delia realised, were holding his hand, she on the left and Jane on the right.

Delia heard their footsteps squelch along the vinyl of the hospital hallway. She turned away from Luke and let go of his hand. Two nurses in white and blue stood in the doorway as she had expected. She didn't recognise their faces but one with rosy cheeks smiled at her and tilted her head as if questioning how this all came about and pitying her.

'It's time,' the rosy cheeked nurse said.

Delia nodded and looked to her mother for reassurance. She

was still asleep in the armchair and didn't rouse. Jane stood, also letting go of Luke's hand. She walked around the bedside and squatted down beside Delia. 'Don't worry,' she said. 'We'll let you know when he wakes up.'

Jane's eyes looked kind. 'I bet you'll be out by spring,' she said.

It seemed unlikely.

'Jane,' Delia said. 'When my mother wakes up can you ask her to come and see me. I have to tell her that I'm sorry.'

She was. For everything.

. . .

Alfred leant over the bed. Luke's eyelids remained closed. He felt Helen's hand on his shoulder as she passed him a cup of coffee.

'When we get out of here I'll sell the orchard,' he said, slumping back into his chair. He raised the cup to his lips and took a sip. The coffee tasted bitter.

Jane, standing by the window, cleared her throat. 'So, I've been thinking about that,' she said. 'I was going to bring it up with you later when we find out what Luke wants to do.'

'I'm not going to push it anymore Jane. He doesn't want to work at the orchard, or take over. He never did. And besides, if he wakes up, he'll probably just leave again.'

Jane's finger tapped at the window sill. 'If?' she questioned. 'No, he'll come right, you'll see, and who knows, maybe this accident will scare him into needing to be closer to home.'

Alfred smiled. 'That's not really how young men work.' He paused, looking up at her. 'So, what was it you were thinking?'

He could see that she looked a little embarrassed.

'I'm not going to be Delia's model anymore. She can find someone else. Luke maybe. She's already been sculpting him.'

241

'Aha. Not sure he'll be keen on that either.'

'I was wondering if I might come and work in the orchard. Just see how it goes.'

He clenched the cup's handle and took another sip. 'You're hoping Luke will come back to the orchard too and that you'll work there together.'

'I'm not hoping that,' her voice started to waver. 'I don't know how any of this is going to turn out.'

Helen spoke up. 'Well, I think it's a good idea Jane. Delia could come and help too when she's out of the ward, stop sculpting for a bit and get those bloody faces out of her head – get some fresh air. Even I'm not destined for the retirement village yet.'

'So that's settled then,' Alfred said. 'The orchard'll be kept ticking over by a model, a mad sculptress and . . .' he looked at Helen.

'And me,' she said. 'You too of course.'

He chuckled and then stopped, returning to look at Luke, then to the floor. The vinyl was the colour of faux polished concrete.

'You've forgotten the lottery money.'

Three heads turned to Luke's bedside to see his eyelids flutter open.

'How much do you need to get out of debt?'

The three stared at him as if he were a ghost, or a statue that shouldn't be able to talk.

'And if it's alright by you –' Luke said '– I'd still like to wander but maybe instead I can come and go. And, I reckon after a few years, maybe I'll get bored of that and come home.'

Alfred thought of the orchard and the breeze passing a maze amongst the trees.

SPRING

A single hawk flew above Aviemore, its silhouette rising to a space beyond sight, untainted by prying eyes. The brushstrokes of frost that clung at the lake's edges had melted away and exposed a variety of earth-toned textures. Off-white stones, the colour of Delia's statues, were submerged at its edge by cool water. Weeping willows dipped and swayed in the currents. The painted stone buried in the water's depths had become hidden by green moss.

Delia sat in the spot where the stone had been cast. Earlier she had hauled all of the statues of Ben, Luke and Jane, one by one, and placed them in a semi-circle around the lake, like guardians. It'd been a big job but she hadn't had to do it on her own. Her skin was oiled with the exertion of it and in the new spring air the sheen began to dry. She visualised the angle of Luke's throw, the length of three skips, the stone hitting the surface and piercing it, falling down. She measured the path of it with her finger and then stood.

Without turning, she removed her clothes, dumped them in a haphazard pile and wove a path back to the lake edge. She waded to above her knees and lowered her body, the chill of the water flowing across her skin colouring her pale blue. She swam gracefully, propelling forward, the cold hiding the ache in her arms. And when she'd reached the spot where she wondered if the stone had landed, she dove.

She arose, turned back towards the side of the lake and smiled. Luke and Jane had shed their clothes too and were running towards the water. She swam to greet them. Then, looking up, she saw Luke's face flicker into a grin. He swam away from them both, further, and further still. Away, as always, away. And then like she had done, he dove below the surface and vanished. She knew what he was looking for and before he rose to the surface, she knew too that he had found it.

Acknowledgements

It is a pleasure to express my gratitude to the many people who helped make this novel possible; to everyone who provided moral support, critique, read, wrote, assisted in the editing, proofreading and design. Thank you to the members of Cloud Ink Press: Annabelle Grierson, Helen McNeil and Dione Jones (project managers for the title), Mark Johnson, Alana Cooke, Anne Kayes and James George.

It is to James George that I bestow utmost thanks. James mentored me during the first two drafts of *Beneath Pale Water*, then called *Powdered Milk* for my Master's thesis in 2015, and further in his position as literary advisor for Cloud Ink Press. He astounds me on a frequent basis with his dedication and drive. He is an excellent creative writing mentor and has taught me so very much.

Thank you to the Auckland University of Technology critique groups that I have been part of; Barbara Else for a manuscript assessment; Lesley Marshall for comprehensive and insightful editing and critique, and Anna Gailani for proofing. Further thanks to Elizabeth Heritage for publicity; Rosa-May Rutherford for cover art and Craig Violich for cover design and typesetting. A huge thank you to Owen Marshall for reading the manuscript and providing a puff quote.

Thank you to my colleagues across three workplaces. Kate Shevland, principal of Orewa College, the Puhoi reading group that Kate is part of, Meryl Howell and the English Department; all staff there; Jenny and Paul at Kip McGrath; Robert Blucher, manager of Te Aho o Te Kura Pounamu, Auckland Branch, the English Department and all my colleagues there too.

I wish to thank my family and the extended arm of my family, my friends. When I was a teenager I used to go to gliding lessons with my late father, Terry Henry in Alexandra and Omarama. One of the most terrifying and amazing experiences I've had was when the instructor looped the glider upside-down and I saw the curve of the earth. It is the setting that I saw from the canopy of the glider that inspired this novel. Thank you to my dad. Thank you to Helen Henry, my mum, who has always encouraged me in all ways, and in this case, to write. Thank you to Jo and Ben Henry. To all extended family. Thank you to my partner, Christopher Kinsler, for moral support, patience, proof reading and cooking, and step children, Dylan and Fergus Kinsler. Thank you to all of my friends, with special note to those that provided feedback for the manuscript: Gillian Wadams, Annie Davis, Nicola Henderson and Jo Rodgers.

Writing a short acknowledgements page isn't easy. Thank you to you all.

About the author

Thalia Henry grew up in Karitane, Otago and features in the *Cloud Ink Press* anthology, *Fresh Ink*. In 2008 she was awarded a place in the *Dunedin Write Out Loud Festival* for her play *Powdered Milk*. She has extended the narrative of that play for this novel, and drawn on inspiration from the landscapes of the rugged South Island high country, where she spent time as a teenager learning to glide with her late father, Terry. *Beneath Pale Water* is her debut novel.